THE MAGICAL STORM

THE MAGICAL STORM

"THE LEGEND OF INKA'S WARRIORS"

Written and Illustrated by:

John Stiles Smith

ISBN: 979-8-218-57039-2

TABLE OF CONTENTS

INTRODUCTION

There's something about Mother Nature that can change a person's world in a month, a day, or even a second.

The Magical Storm is an Arizona story about a massive dust storm (Haboob) that possesses the power to time travel and the storm's interactions with three thirteen-year-old boys who are best friends.

The Magical Storm forges a destiny with our young friends and creates journeys for a reason, returning the boys home for a purpose. But for the boys to bring a positive change to humanity, they must overcome challenges and obstacles to survive and succeed.

It's not just an Arizona story, it's a story about facing the odds, doing the right thing, and having the determination to be triumphant. Our boys must work together to carry out their destiny, making a difference one storm at a time.

CHAPTER ONE

THE BOYS

Under bright sunny skies sits a single-story classic Arizona Ranch home. In the background, a red horse barn augments the property. Mesquite trees dot the acre or so front yard, and Mexican palm trees line a long gravel driveway. A couple of saguaro cacti fill the landscape. A pickup truck with a two-horse trailer is parked along a three-tiered, white wooden rail fence. At the front of the driveway above the entrance gate, an arched sign reads The Garcia Horse Ranch. The Garcia family has been in Arizona for generations, and a look at the surroundings tells you these folks know horses.

A cloud of dust and dirt kicks up as thirteen-year-old JJ Garcia busts horse hooves around a barrel at the family ranch's makeshift horse barrel-racing course.

"Come on, Sadie, dig it in, girl!" an encouraging JJ shouts.

JJ rhythmically strides in the saddle. His long black hair and brown vest waft in the breeze. His cowboy boots move with each gallop. He wears blue jeans most of the time as his legs hug Sadie's body. JJ looks determined and knows how important it is to post a good time. He pushes Sadie around a barrel, then races to the next barrel. Hooves pound and dirt flies as JJ guides Sadie around the final barrel. Her head is low, and her body looks powerful with her big leg muscles working hard, but she is graceful as she carries JJ through his morning practice run. His parents, Dan and Sheila, along with his twelve-year-old sister, Amy, enthusiastically cheer JJ on. Next to the family, JJ's dog Lucky watches the action.

"Let's go, JJ!" his mom shouts.

JJ's dad anxiously checks his stopwatch, then stares out toward JJ with a tense look.

"You're running a great time, JJ, but push her, you got to push her!" JJ's dad shouts.

Dan checks his stopwatch as Amy is wildly jumping up and down with her fists in the air.

"Come on, JJ!" screams Amy, who will be having her own practice later that day. Dan keeps a tight grip on his stopwatch and a close eye on JJ. Dan is all business.

"Hug the barrel, son. You got to push her harder!" Dan yells. JJ leans forward close to Sadie's ear. Sadie is a horse JJ has grown up with and loves.

"Go, Sadie, come on, girl," JJ says, directing Sadie through the morning workout.

JJ has that special knack with animals. Not only the ability to communicate but also to understand an animal's feeling and fears.

Sadie responds. Hooves aggressively pound the ground as dirt flies, and Sadie grunts loudly as she gives it her all. They approach the final barrel and cut a sharp, tight turn. Rounding the barrel, JJ and Sadie charge toward the finish line. Something else about JJ is that he's a natural leader and one of the best young horsemen in Arizona. He loves the history of the various Native American tribes in the southwest United States, especially tribes with a history from the central Arizona region.

Dan takes a quick glance at his stopwatch. Sheila and Amy watch JJ's final streak home.

"Finish strong, JJ, finish strong!" Dan yells, checking his stopwatch one last time.

JJ and Sadie blast past the finish line, followed by a trail of dust and dirt. Dan's lips tighten as he shakes his head. It's obvious he is disappointed as he stares off, really looking at nothing but deep in thought.

JJ is sporting a big smile as he trots up to his father. He immediately senses his dad's disappointment, and his smile leaves his face as he waits for his dad's response to the practice run. Dan gives JJ a serious look. You know the look, that

"I'm not happy" look.

"Son…you're going to have to push Sadie harder if you want to bring a trophy back to the ranch," Dan says with a stern look and then stares off. He looks at JJ while he tucks the stopwatch into his back pocket.

"A trophy is money, son. It sells horses," Dan says while letting out a big sigh. "We're in the business to sell horses, just remember that," he says as he walks away.

JJ reaches down and pats Lucky on the head. JJ's mom gives him an encouraging look.

"You did great, JJ. You'll be ready for the state rodeo championship, I know you will!" says JJ's mom as reassuringly as she can be. He gives his mom a smile.

"I'll be ready," JJ says as he pets Sadie. "I mean, we'll be ready, won't we, girl?" He continues to pet Sadie, then quickly looks for his mom.

"Mom!" JJ calls out, and she stops and looks at JJ.

"Yes, JJ?" she answers.

"Sadie and I are going for a ride, and then I'm meeting Brad and Calvin for a hike later, okay?" JJ asks.

"Sure, JJ, you've earned it, be careful and have fun," Sheila replies. "And when you get back, I'll give you a ride to meet your friends."

"I will," JJ says. He gives the reins a gentle tug and turns Sadie around. Then, like a rocket, they blast off, charging across the horse yard straight toward a fence in the opposite direction.

"Hyah, hyah!" JJ shouts. He presses Sadie to pick up the pace. "Hyah, hyah." Sadie pounds hooves as she charges toward the fence. JJ is riding low in the saddle close to Sadie's neck. They both stride in rhythm as if they are one object as they get closer to the fence. Then, with only several feet from the fence, JJ gives her the command.

"Jump, Sadie!" JJ shouts. Sadie responds with grace and beauty as she takes to the air. Airborne, she sails over the fence and lands effortlessly. JJ gives Sadie a rub on the top of her head.

"Good girl," JJ says. He gives the reins a slight tug, and they gallop off toward the open desert.

"Hyah, hyah!" JJ shouts as his voice fades away in the desert.

There is a loud bang as a body wearing a white karate outfit slams down onto a blue practice mat. Meet Bradley Thompson, known to his friends as Brad. Brad's face winces in pain as his medium-length blond hair follows him to the mat.

"Ugh!" Brad grunts as he stares straight up, which reveals his blue eyes. Brad is training for his black belt, something he promised his dad who is somewhere along the Afghanistan-Pakistan border.

Brad is big for his age, he is not the brightest kid, but he is very athletic. A Chicago transplant who is extremely loyal to his friends. In other words, you mess with JJ or Calvin, you mess with Brad. He especially has Calvin's back, ever since they met in third grade.

Brad stands up and adjusts his brown belt. He gets into a martial art fighting position. He readies himself and looks determined.

Standing next to the mat is Brad's karate instructor. He wears the traditional white karate uniform with a black belt tied at the waist. His hands are folded behind his back, and you can sense his frustration with Brad's performance today.

"Mr. Thompson, twice you have had the opportunity to defeat a large opponent…confidence, Mr. Thompson, confidence," the instructor says.

Brad places his feet together and lowers his hands to his side. He respectfully bows his head.

"Yes, sensei," Brad replies.

The instructor walks away as soft footsteps echo in the dojo. He opens the door to his office, then stops and turns around with a compassionate but a stern look at Brad.

"Mr. Thompson, I know you want to earn a black belt for your father, that is very honorable, but there's a lesson my sensei taught me that you should learn," the instructor says.

Brad is curious and slightly raises his head. The instructor continues.

"He called it…own the moment. In life you must understand when you need to own the moment," the instructor says as the door closes.

Brad's blue eyes search the room as he ponders the state-ment. "Own the moment?" Brad mutters to himself. "What does that mean?" Brad scratches his head and doesn't quite get it. Puzzled, he looks around the room for an answer, then shrugs his shoulders.

"Oh well, I got to meet the guys," Brad says. He darts off, and within seconds, a door slams.

It's a beautiful sunny blue sky, and suddenly a gray re-mote-controlled airplane, which resembles a World War II P-51 Mustang Fighter with the classic white star in the center of a blue disk, screams straight toward the ground.

Near impact, the plane transitions into a tight 360-degree loop. Oohs and aahs from a crowd hint at their excitement. The plane descends to land. In the background on a fence, a banner reads 2017, Arizona Eagle Scout 1st Annual So-lar-Powered Airplane Contest.

Above the sign a crowd of about fifty spectators break into a standing ovation and enthusiastically applaud and cheer. In the center of a fenced-off thirty-by-sixty-yard out-door arena stands thirteen-year-old Calvin Jackson. Calvin is operating the remote control with a perfect touch.

Let me tell you something about Calvin, he's a genius and a gadget freak. He can build anything, but he especially loves to build things that fly. He wears gold aviator glasses and sports a four-inch twisted Afro with trimmed sides. Calvin is always Eagle Scout ready. His standard attire is a khaki short-sleeve shirt and shorts with ankle-high hiking boots. And he always carries a black backpack full of almost everything you would need to build something. Today, Calvin is motivated to earn a merit badge to fill his Eagle Scout sash.

The plane with a wingspan of four feet taxis on the ground followed by a slight trail of dust. The plane rumbles up to Calvin. He has an earbud with a small microphone that's connected to a walkie-talkie clipped to his belt. Calvin adjusts the knob on the walkie-talkie.

"Great flying, son, twenty on and one more to go!" Calvin's dad says enthusiastically through the earbud.

Calvin proudly stands by his plane and eyes his scout sash full of merit badges. He sports a big smile knowing he's going to place well in the contest.

"Well, folks, how about those moves!" the contest announcer says through a PA system. "That was Calvin Jackson from Phoenix, Arizona, and it looks like Calvin is the winner today. Let's give Calvin a big hand!" The crowd is still on their feet and amp up the applause and cheering.

Calvin pushes his glasses up off his nose and waves to the crowd.

"Wow, this is awesome!" Calvin says. "Well, better meet my parents."

In the parking lot next to a newer model Ford Explorer

are Calvin's parents. Tom and Sunny-Kim Jackson, both computer engineers and New York City transplants. The parents wear the same khaki outfits as Calvin. Calvin is kneeling on the ground disassembling his airplane. He rolls up a six-by-twelve-inch solar panel and sets it by his backpack, along with the walkie-talkies.

"I think I'll do an inventory check before repacking my backpack," Calvin mutters as he turns his backpack upside down, and a variety of stuff tumbles out.

"Binoculars, duct tape, heavy gauge string, check… Three-way compass, which includes a reflecting mirror and a magnifying glass, check, and Swiss army knife, check," Calvin says with a big smile as he admires his goods.

"Supplies in order," Calvin says as he begins to repack his backpack.

Tom, in his customary fashion, pushes his glasses up off his nose and directs his attention to Calvin.

"Calvin, when you're ready, we'll give you a ride to the hiking trail," Tom says.

Calvin stuffs the remote control and motor into his backpack and gives his dad a smile.

"Thanks, Dad," Calvin replies. He is excited to go hiking and to hang out with his best friends.

So the boys are off and will meet each other for their afternoon hike, a favorite activity of exploring a vast mountain range know as South Mountain. It's a conglomeration of three different ranges: the Ma Ha Tauk, the Gila, and the

Guadalupe. The ranges were formed fifteen to twenty-five million years ago when the earth's lower layer, known as continental plates, collided, pushing various forms of rock through the surface of the earth to impressive elevations.

Chapter Two

THE STORM

JJ is standing at the edge of the trailhead parking lot. He's tossing rocks out into the desert. He is half daydreaming and half thinking about the upcoming rodeo tournament as he patiently waits for his friends. The sound of an approaching vehicle gets his attention; he turns around.

Calvin's parents pull up in their Ford Explorer next to JJ. The driver's window goes down revealing Calvin's dad. JJ waves.

"Hi, Mr. and Mrs. Jackson," JJ says.

Tom smiles and waves back to JJ. Calvin's mom leans forward and waves. Calvin jumps out of the passenger side back seat and flings his backpack on. He briskly walks behind the vehicle and up to JJ.

"Hey, JJ," Tom says. "Now, Calvin, don't forget you have

the awards ceremony tonight."

Calvin snaps to attention and conducts a casual three-finger Eagle Scout salute.

"No worries, Pops," Calvin responds.

The window goes up, and the SUV pulls away. JJ and Calvin share a smile and a fist bump, their standard greeting.

"So, where's Brad?" Calvin asks. "Late as usual?" Calvin says in a sarcastic tone. JJ shrugs his shoulders.

"What else in new? It's Brad," JJ replies. A horn beeps, and the two boys look across the parking lot. A light-blue Ford Mustang pulls into the parking lot. The vehicle pulls up to JJ and Calvin. The passenger door opens, and Brad jumps out. He's wearing his standard attire, an off-white, number 42 baseball jersey. It's unbuttoned over a white tank top, along with blue jeans and gym shoes. Another characteristic of Brad, he always wears a Chicago Cubs hat on backward.

The driver's tinted window rolls down revealing Brad's mom, Cindy Thompson. She gives JJ and Calvin a friendly wave.

"Hi, JJ. Hi, Calvin," Cindy says. The boys return the wave.

"Hi, Mrs. Thompson," JJ and Calvin reply together. Her smiling face turns serious as she directs her eyes on Brad.

"Now, Brad, don't be late for dinner. And look out for rattlesnakes!" Brad's mom commands. Brad shrugs his shoulders and sports an innocent face.

"Me, late for dinner? Never!" Brad says. "Bye, Mom." The window rolls up, and the car drives away.

Brad playfully shimmies and struts his way up to JJ and Calvin.

"Dudes!" a happy Brad says. "Are you ready to pound some ground?" Within seconds, Brad and Calvin catch eyes and immediately squint like a couple of gunslingers. They get into a gun-draw position and act out a pretend tense moment. Each slightly nods their head, indicating they're ready to play a common game almost themselves.

"Rock, paper, scissors, shoot!" Calvin and Brad shout together. In a wink of an eye, Calvin throws paper, but Brad to his jubilation throws scissors.

"Scissors, I win!" Brad yells. "Looks like you're hauling the backpack, Calvin," Brad says as he digs it in. Calvin flashes a smirk on his face and grabs the backpack strap with a slight tug.

"Yeah, I'll get you next time," Calvin responds. JJ, who has been watching these two toy with each other for years, just smiles and shakes his head. He points to the trail.

"You two ready?" JJ asks as he walks away, leading the way. JJ pretty much always takes the lead.

So, the boys start their long-awaited hike on a trail known as Telegraph Pass. The first part of their journey will be a little over a mile and will take them to a location called the Eagle's Nest, a shelter built in the 1930s. Along the way, JJ will be looking for ancient petroglyph, stone carvings on rock formations left by the Hohokam thousands of years ago. Brad, as always, will be searching for arrowheads, and Calvin will be absorbing everything. He'll calculate it, think about it, and store whatever away in his brain for another time.

JJ continues to lead the way. Calvin and Brad josh with each other, another common occurrence between the two. A harmless push here and an elbow smack there but all in fun. Ahead of them, the trail fades away into a vast mountainous desert. Saguaros and ocotillo cacti are scattered throughout the landscape along with colorful wildflowers. On top of the mountain, there is an assortment of tall communication towers.

Brad stops and looks down toward the ground. His eyes get wide, and he thinks found something, maybe an arrowhead. Brad stops and picks the object up as JJ and Calvin continue to hike up the trail. He examines his discovery with a close eye.

"Nope, not an arrowhead," Brad mutters to himself. He takes a closer look and appears puzzled as he scratches the back of his neck.

"This looks like a seashell," Brad mutters. "A seashell?" He looks up and sees he is lagging, but he is still curious about his findings.

"Dudes, I think I found a seashell. What's it doing up here?" Brad asks. JJ and Calvin stop to turn around.

"That's because four hundred million years ago, a time that was called the Devonian Period, Arizona was under water!" Calvin responds. "Also known as the Age of Fishes!" Calvin adds.

Brad shrugs his shoulders and tosses the seashell out into the desert.

"You don't say, Mister Know-It-All," Brad sarcastically replies. Calvin flashes his palms out and shakes his head.

"I'm just saying," Calvin says.

JJ is checking things out, knowing there's plenty of trail ahead.

"Hurry up, Brad!" JJ says. "We got a lot of land to cover!" Brad takes off in a jog to catch up as JJ and Calvin patiently wait for their friend.

Calvin whips his backpack around and pulls out his binoculars. He hangs them around his neck, then lifts them under his glasses to his eyes. Calvin scans the surroundings, seeing desert landscape and a hint of mountains on the southern horizon. Moving his view closer, he sees housetops, trees, and the local school grounds. Down the street, traffic passes through the intersection. A closer view reveals cactus, sage bushes, and desert ground. Calvin scans the ground near him, and suddenly a large scorpion fills his lens. If there's something that chills Calvin, it's a scorpion.

"Aah!" Calvin screams. Simultaneously in a panic, he jumps into Brad's arms. Brad is caught by surprise but makes the catch and stumbles backward. Then like a comic series, Brad crashes into JJ's head and whacks him right in the nose. JJ's cowboy hat flies off his head as JJ stumbles to the ground, landing on his butt.

"What's going on?" a perturb JJ cries. JJ grabs his nose and gets off the ground. He picks up his hat and pounds it against his leg, knocking the dust off. Meanwhile, Brad is still holding Calvin, who sheepishly points in the direction of the would-be scorpion.

"Geez, a scorpion, it looked huge through the binoculars. Those things give me the willies!" Calvin replies while still pointing. "It's over there."

"I don't see it, guess there's not too many scorpions in the Big Apple, huh, Calvin?" JJ responds.

"Man, I just can't get used to those things. They're freaky, and they creep me out!" Calvin says with a bit of a street tone in his voice.

"Get used to them, you're the visitor," JJ replies. JJ, while still holding his nose, starts to walk away, shaking his head in a disturbed manner.

"The two of you," JJ scoffs.

"Whatever, they're still creepy!" Calvin responds. Brad gives Calvin a grin, a kind of "Really, dude?" look.

"So, do you think it's safe yet?" Brad says in a sarcastic tone. Calvin looks at Brad and rolls his eyes.

"Please," Calvin responds.

Brad gives Calvin a gentle toss, and he lands on his feet. Calvin and Brad fist bump and share a smile. They hustle up to JJ, and the boys resume their hike.

It's later in the day. The boys are hiking at a much higher

elevation. The sun is shining, and all is well. Then suddenly almost out of nowhere, the wind picks up and a slight howling sound begins to fill the air. JJ's and Brad's hair start to waft in the breeze. In a manner of a few seconds, dust and debris start to blow, and the sunlight dims.

JJ, somewhat puzzled, looks out toward the southern horizon and gets wide-eyed and appears startled.

"Wow!" an excited JJ yells. "Looks what's coming!"

The boys stare off with slack-jawed expressions as if totally caught in awe as a massive wall of dust rolls across the southern horizon. Like a giant tidal wave with the wind and quickly getting stronger, the massive wall of dust is traveling straight toward the boys' location.

"Holy guacamole!" Calvin shouts. "That's the biggest haboob I've ever seen!" Brad gives Calvin a dumbfounded look.

"A what?" Brad says. Calvin gives Brad a quick glance, then stares back out toward the massive wall of dust storm. He looks at Brad again.

"A haboob," Calvin responds over the increasing howling of the wind. Calvin, who is never someone to shy away from his intelligence, pushes his glasses up off his nose.

"Just for the record, a haboob, by definition, is a violent dust storm," Calvin lectures. "Very characteristic of the Middle East, Australia, and the Southwest, you know… Arizona," Calvin says. JJ's hair is blowing wildly as he pushes his cowboy hat down for a tighter fit.

"Let me tell you, I've seen plenty, but this one looks real nasty!" JJ interjects. And he was right, this haboob was like no other. It towered a mile high with winds gusting between fifty to seventy miles per hour. It was massive, stretching across the entire valley, and it was heading straight toward the boys.

Brad starts to act anxious; he's the fidgety type when he gets nervous. He starts to quickly look around, getting ready to make his move.

"Well, holy whatever, it's scary looking!" Brad yells. "Let's get out of here!" Brad can't take it any longer and begins to run. JJ grabs Brad by his shirt collar and pulls him back. JJ gives Brad and Calvin a serious look.

"It's too late, and this storm is moving like a freight train. We need to find some shelter and fast!" JJ hollers. That's what is steady about JJ. He's scared like Calvin and Brad, who are in a near panic mode, but JJ keeps his cool. He's learned from riding horses at a fast gallop you got to keep your head and think clearly.

So, they dart away like bullets. JJ leads the way, scanning for shelter and protection from the onslaught of the storm. The moment is tense and very dangerous. Dust, debris, and small rocks are blasting through the air at great velocity. But this storm is different and has arrived for a reason to form a destiny with JJ, Calvin, and Brad. Unknown to our friends, they will become part of something that's bigger than themselves. Their destiny will have a purpose in life and for the betterment of humanity, but at this moment, the boys must survive the storm.

JJ spots a large boulder and signals to Calvin and Brad to hurry and follow him. They quickly dash behind the boulder and take shelter as the dust and debris violently blows havoc on the mountain. The howling is deafening, and the ground is shaking.

"Stay together and keep your eyes closed!" JJ yells.

Within seconds the massive wall of dust engulfs the boulder. The dust is so thick the boulder vanishes from view, and nothing is visible. The wall of dust from the storm was so huge that the highest point on South Mountain, elevation 2690 feet above sea level, had also disappeared. The storm dwarfed the mountain. All the boys could do was huddle and hope.

And just as the intensity of the wind couldn't howl any louder and the wind couldn't blow any stronger, the storm starts to ease up. Gradually, the howling fades, and the large boulder comes into view. Almost like a light switch, the wind is gone, and the sun is shining.

The boys step out from behind the large boulder. Brad brushes some dirt off his Cubs hat and then some more dirt off his baseball jersey. He spits some dirt out of his mouth.

"Dudes, that was some storm dust!" Brad proclaims as JJ and Calvin brush dirt off their clothing.

"You can say that again," Calvin responds. Brad gives Calvin a half-serious look as if Calvin really wants him to repeat his statement. He shrugs his shoulders.

"Dudes, that was some dust storm!" Brad repeats.

Calvin just shakes his head and rolls his eyes. He notices JJ is scanning the area with a very precarious or uncertain face and finds JJ's demeanor unusual.

"What's wrong, JJ?" Calvin asks. JJ continues to scan the surroundings with a puzzled expression. Calvin and Brad are totally unaware what JJ is about to show them. JJ points in the direction of the neighborhood.

"Look!" JJ shouts in a very anxious tone. Calvin and Brad look out toward the direction JJ is pointing. They look confused and bewildered; they share a glance.

"Huh!" Calvin mutters.

"Hey, what happened?" Brad asks. JJ continues his search for something normal.

So the boys stare out toward their neighborhood only to see a vast desert and no signs of any familiar landmarks. No houses, no streets, and no school grounds—for the boys' neighborhood has vanished.

Calvin and Brad continue to stare out with blank faces. JJ gives them a somber look.

"I don't know what happened," JJ answers. "Let's get to the top of the mountain for a better look!" JJ says. The boys share a head nod in agreement and dash away, charging up the trail that should have taken them to Eagle's Nest, but that has all changed.

JJ and Brad reach the top of the mountain, each panting heavily. Calvin was lagging but shortly makes his way alongside his friends. He's bent over with his hands on his knees trying to catch his breath. Together the three boys stare out into the valley. They share a glance and look worried.

The view is the same, desert landscape for miles and no signs of modern civilization. Brad rubs his forehead in confusion as JJ just shakes his head in disbelief. The boys can't get a handle on what happened. Calvin decides to take a better look and grabs his binoculars that are still hanging from his neck. He scans the valley, then lowers the binoculars and squints his eyes. He brings the binoculars to his eyes again but quickly lowers them and appears puzzled.

"JJ, you need to see this!" Calvin says.

JJ anxiously grabs the binoculars that are hanging from Calvin's neck.

"Agh!" Calvin grunts. "Let me out!" He slips off the strap and frees himself. JJ brings the binoculars to his eyes and focuses on the direction of Calvin's curiosity.

In view surrounded by desert and bushes is a small village of adobe-style houses positioned close to a large, steep rock formation, much like a huge square boulder. In the center of the village, a trail of smoke curls into the sky. From the distance the village looks peaceful and maybe, perhaps welcoming. JJ continues to scan the area while Calvin and Brad share a puzzled look. They wonder what JJ is seeing and if it means help is near.

"What do you see, JJ?" Calvin asks in a curious tone as

JJ keeps the binoculars in place.

"That's strange, two-story adobe houses," JJ mutters in a soft tone. "Hmm, it looks like a Hopi Indian village."

Brad rears his head back totally bewildered and is taken aback by JJ's comment.

"A what?!" Brad asks.

JJ lowers the binoculars and gives Calvin and Brad a serious look.

"Hundreds of years ago, we know certain Native American tribes lived and farmed near the Salt River," JJ says. He pauses and stares out toward the village. "Right where that smoke is coming from."

Brad starts to get jittery, and Calvin looks deeply worried. They both are feeling something has gone wrong.

"What's going on?" Brad asks. "I can't be late for dinner!"

JJ continues to just stare out toward the village. His face looks somber, but he's in deep thought. JJ knows something big has happened.

"It's like we're back in time…as if the storm had magical powers!" JJ proclaims. Calvin is nervously looking around.

"Man, I can't be back in time!" Calvin yells in his street tone.

Brad starts to pace nervously in a small circle as he rubs his forehead. He gives JJ a desperate look.

"Time traveled. What are you talking about? I've got a karate lesson in the morning!" Brad anxiously says. "My mom's going to kill me!" Calvin and Brad share a desperate look, then simultaneously grab their phones and frantically start pushing buttons. Calvin gives his cell phone a puzzled look.

"Huh…no service," Calvin mutters. Brad looks at Calvin, then at his cell phone.

"You're kidding me, no service!" Brad yells. Calvin and Brad share panicked looks and nervously resume pushing their cell phone buttons.

JJ holds the binoculars to his chest and blankly stares out toward the village. Meanwhile Calvin and Brad are beside themselves and quite upset about the cell phone issue.

"What's up with these cell phones?" Brad says. "I knew I should have changed services!" Brad continues.

JJ points to the top of South Mountain where the communication towers used to be.

"Forget!" JJ says. "There's no towers, no satellites, no cables or anything!" JJ walks away and looks out toward the southern horizon. Suddenly, as if something has caught his eye, he curiously squints and grabs the binoculars. JJ starts to scan the southern horizon. He lowers the binoculars and wipes the lens. He looks puzzled and raises the binoculars to his eyes.

In view out toward the southern horizon, a large trail of dust is moving in the direction toward the western area of the South Mountain range. Faintly coming into view is a hint of men on horses through the dust cloud. Calvin and Brad have stopped fussing about their cell phones, they get it, but now their curiosity is focused on JJ. They walk over to JJ to see what he has been looking at.

"What is it?" Calvin asks.

JJ adjusts the binoculars for a better view. He addresses Calvin and Brad as he continues his observation.

"Strange, but it looks like soldiers," JJ answers. "I can see some on horses, some on foot, and a couple of wagons," JJ continues. Calvin's and Brad's eyes light up. They're excited, hoping for the best.

"This is great, a rescue party!" Brad says as he fist pumps the sky with excitement.

"Just what we need, I'll flag them down!" Calvin proclaims.

"Nah, they're too far away; besides, I don't think they're any rescue party," JJ says. He lowers the binoculars and rubs his eyes. He appears puzzled and raises the binoculars to his eyes for another look.

"Fellas!" JJ shouts. "You're not going to believe this, that cloud of dust almost looks like a group of Spanish conquistadors!" he adds.

JJ lowers the binoculars and shares a bewildered look with Calvin and Brad. The boys' hopeful faces have now been transformed to gloom and confusion.

25

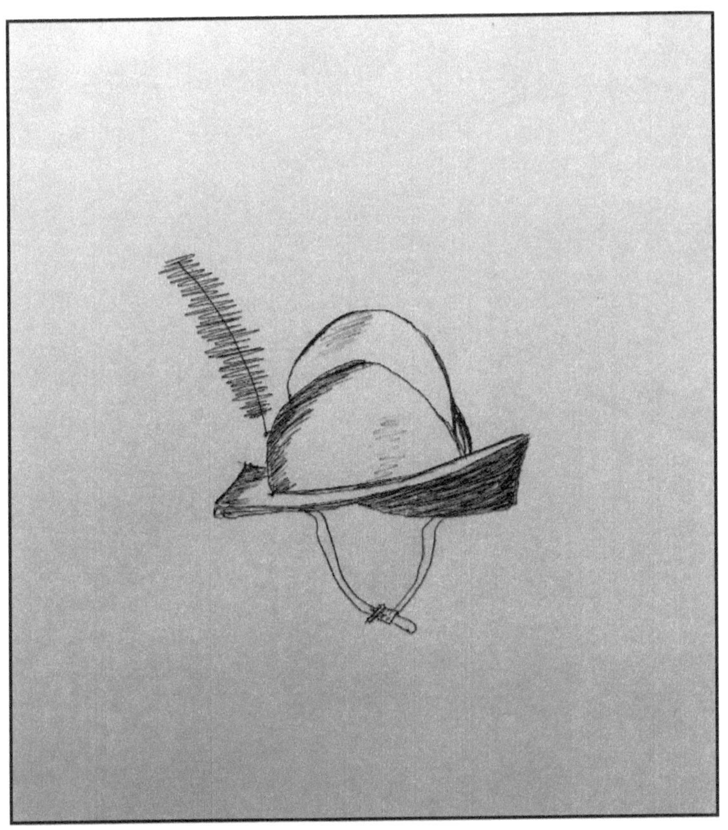

Chapter Three

THE CONQUISTADORS

Trotting out of the haze from a cloud of dust are six Spanish conquistadors wearing full battle armor. Behind the horse soldiers and emerging out of the cloud of dust are a dozen foot soldiers marching in a two-man column. Trailing the foot soldiers are two horse-drawn wagons that are empty. They are traveling north toward a passageway that will take them to the valley flatlands.

JJ follows the soldiers with the binoculars as Calvin and Brad quizzically stare out toward the soldiers.

"Spanish conquistadors?" JJ mutters in a curious voice.

Brad rears his head and appears very confused.

"Spanish conquistadors!" Brad responds. "I thought that was a soccer team."

Calvin continues to stare out in the direction of the soldiers with a blank face. He squints his eyes and looks at JJ.

"Where do you think they're going?" Calvin asks. JJ is still tracking the soldiers with the binoculars.

"I don't know, but they're almost to the mountain passageway," JJ informs Calvin. The three boys share puzzled expressions and can only wonder what is going on. The soldiers and the two wagons vanish out of view. They have traveled directly to the passageway as if they knew there was a separation where the South Mountain range ends at the western point and east of the Sierra Estrella Mountain range. The soldiers were out of sight for the moment, leaving the boys puzzled and worried.

"Hmm," JJ quietly mutters. "A Hopi tribe and Spanish conquistadors…we must be back in time around the mid-sixteenth century," JJ says in a curious voice.

Well, that's all Calvin and Brad needed to hear. The panic in their faces quickly returns as they exchange both frightened and dumbfounded expression, then stare out toward the desert.

"The mid-sixteenth century!" Calvin yells. He gives JJ a desperate look. "What about my merit badge?" an excited Calvin says.

"No way!" Brad shouts. "I promised my dad I'd earn a black belt!" Brad continues. The boys look anxious with hopeless faces. Calvin and Brad lean on JJ when something is wrong or doesn't feel right, and they look at JJ for leadership.

"Look, let's head to the north side of the mountain

and see where they're going," JJ suggests. The boys share a head nod and quickly dart away toward the north side for a better view. The north side of the mountain is only about fifty yards away, and the location will allow the boys to see the soldiers as they emerge out of the northern portion of the passageway to territory several miles west of the village.

The boys are gathered and are scanning the west valley, waiting for the soldiers to come into view. The moment is tense, and the boys don't know what to expect when suddenly JJ squints his eyes and quickly brings the binoculars into play.

"I see them!" an excited JJ yells. He fine-tunes the binoculars.

In view, the conquistadors steadily appear coming out of the north side of the passageway. They're led by a soldier on a horse who wears a more colorful uniform and a large red feather attached to his helmet. The red feather indicates he is the captain of the soldiers. Following behind him is a soldier with a large black feather attached to his helmet. This means he is the captain's lieutenant. Grouped closely behind the lieutenant and trotting in a neat orderly fashion are five additional horse soldiers. Keeping pace behind the five horse soldiers are a dozen foot soldiers. They have maintained their discipline and continue to march in a two-man column. And bringing up the rear are the two empty horse-drawn wagons.

JJ lowers the binoculars and gives Calvin and Brad a

serious look.

"Fellas, they're conquistadors all right, and they look mean and dangerous!" an anxious JJ says. He pauses and ponders the situation. Suddenly he gets wide-eyed as if he realizes what may be taking place.

"And it looks like they're headed straight toward the village!" JJ adds in a striking manner. Calvin and Brad have noticed JJ's demeanor, and it has caught their attention. They know JJ, and they know when something doesn't feel right with him.

"Should we do something?" Calvin asks. Brad's eyes light up, and he feels a ray of hope.

"Dudes, maybe if we warn them, they could help us get home!" Brad adds. The boys share a glance. The kind of look where they're all on same page and thinking the same.

"Maybe… Look, it's only a few miles so let's go!" JJ says. They share a head nod and dart down a northern trail as fast as they can. The boys are hoping they can get to the village in time to warn them of the approaching danger.

Meanwhile, outside the village and out of view of the villagers, the conquistadors have lined up in an attack formation. The lieutenant is positioned front and center as he waits for his orders. The foot soldiers have formed a straight twelve-man line with two horse soldiers at each end to guard the flanks, or sides. A single horse soldier remains behind the foot soldiers to back the rear and to make sure no one retreats. The soldiers are quiet and steadfast.

The conquistador captain trots his horse in front of the formation, inspecting his troops. The red feather on his helmet bounces with each step of the horse; abruptly he pulls the reins and stops. The captain's eyes scan the formation with a face that means business.

"Men, we have traveled far, and soon we'll be rewarded!" shouts the captain. His right hand grabs the handle of his sword that's strapped to his left side. He aggressively draws the weapon and raises it over his head while positioning his horse toward the village.

"Attack!" the captain yells. As if well-rehearsed, the soldiers quickly move lockstep toward the village. The sunlight shines off their armor making them almost appear like a mirage and very difficult for anyone to see the advancing onslaught. The soldiers are only about fifty yards outside the village and have maintained their disciplined march. Suddenly the captain looks back on his troops and raises his sword as high as he can.

"Charge!" the captain shouts. The troops break formation and run with weapons drawn.

The village's two-story adobe homes form a horseshoe pattern with the houses arcing around the west side and a large, steep rock formation on the east side. The villagers are unaware of the approaching danger. The men are working on the soil in the village farm, and the women can be seen carrying firewood to their homes. Children run freely and play in the center of the village. The atmosphere embellishes the meaning of the word Hopi, which means peaceful.

Suddenly the ground starts to tremor, and faint yelling can be heard. Some of the men stop their work and curiously look out toward the west. Then, without warning, the conquistadors storm the village. The attack is swift, and the Hopi men are caught off guard.

It's utter chaos as the villagers run for their lives. Screams and cries fill the air. The men try to fight, but they have no weapons and are quickly overtaken by the surprise. The situation is dire. A half hour later, the boys finally make to the outskirts of the village. They slowly sneak up behind some bushes and are still panting hard from the run. They look out in awe at the events in front of them as the soldiers rampage the village. The boys feel sad, especially JJ. He's the kind that would carry the burden of a failed effort and is feeling that weight now.

"We're too late!" a despondent JJ says.

They share somber looks and helplessly watch as they slowly keep moving to avoid being seen. Step-by-step they continue to advance closer to the center of the village. They know that if caught, it could be death.

In the village the turmoil continues. A mean-faced beard-ed soldier who is encased in full body armor steps into the center of the village as he searches for more prisoners. His fist is clenched, and he has a sword in his other hand. An arrow suddenly strikes his chest armor and harmlessly falls to the ground. The soldier flashes a sarcastic grin and laughs, then charges away. The village men are being rounded up; some continue to fight bravely but are no match against the heavily armored intruders.

Two soldiers aggressively push one of the village men toward a stockade full of prisoners. Other soldiers continue chasing the remaining village men as the women and children frantically run in all directions. The attack is swift and ruth-less with each minute bringing the village into submission.

The conquistador captain charges on his horse into the center of the village, his red feather flopping with each gal-lop. He pulls the reins, stopping his horse, and dismounts. There's nothing nice about this man.

"Get me the village chief!" the captain demands.

Two soldiers each hold an upper arm of an Indian man who is in his early fifties. He is the village chief, and unlike the other village men who wear a simple breechcloth, the chief wears a sarong. A sarong is a long piece of fabric that is worn around the waist. It's made from cotton, which was grown near the village. Also, he is wearing a gold medallion necklace.

"Are you the village chief?" asks the captain in a very

aggressive tone.

"Yes, I'm the village chief, and these are my people!" the chief snaps back. "Why have you come here?!" the chief asks. The captain rears his head back as if taken by the forcefulness of the voice. He squints his eyes and gives the chief an angry stare.

"I'll ask the questions here!" the captain snaps back.

The boys continue to sneak closer to the center of the village using the bushes for cover. JJ hand gestures he's going to look and slowly raises his head over the top of a bush. Calvin and Brad are anxious as they watch JJ. They share a nervous glance and look back at JJ.

"What are they saying?" Calvin asks.

"Can't tell, but it seems like they're trying to get information from one of the village men," JJ responds.

The conquistador captain notices the gold medallion hanging from the village chief's neck. The captain squints his eyes, then suddenly he rips the medallion from the chief's neck.

"Where did you get this?!" the captain demands.

"That is not yours to know!" the defiant chief responds.

"I have come a long ways!" shouts the captain. "And I want answers!" The captain grows angry and impatient with the chief.

"Tell me or I'll get my answers the…hard way," says the captain. He grabs the handle of his sword, and in an intimidating fashion, he slowly lifts it up and down while in the sheath.

The village chief glances at the gold medallion in the captain's hand. He notices a scar on the captain's forearm. The chief rears his head and gets wide-eyed as he stares at the scar as if it has brought back old feelings. The captain curiously watches the chief's reaction but doesn't quite understand why the chief is acting the way he is. He ponders his next move and realizes he must pursue his immediate object and doesn't have time for the defiant village chief. He looks at the guards and points toward the large, steep rock formation. Near the bottom of the rock formation there's a long ledge approximately ten feet from the ground and twenty feet wide. Near the center of the ledge, a tall wooden post has been installed and is used to dry deer hides.

"Take him to that post and tie him up!" the captain shouts as he points to the post. "I'll deal with him later."

The two soldiers push the village chief away as soldiers chase down the last remaining villagers. Screams and cries still echo throughout the village. The captain appears puzzled and rubs his chin in curiosity.

"Those eyes…I have seen those eyes before," the captain ponders, "but…where?" he mutters to himself. The captain stares off and wonders why he is having such feelings.

36

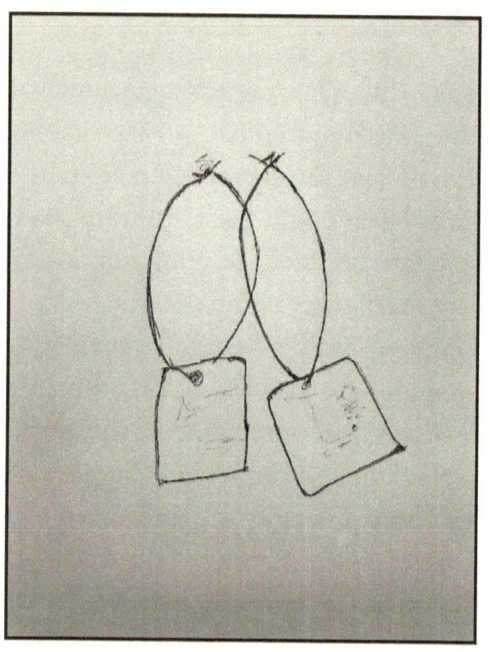

Chapter Four

PRINCESS INKA AND THE GOLD MEDALLION MAPS

JJ, Calvin, and Brad are quietly lurking behind the bushes and have remained unnoticed throughout the rampage. Then suddenly a bush next to the boys begins to rustle. JJ slowly brings his index finger to his lips.

"Shh…," JJ quietly mutters. Then he signals for Calvin and Brad to separate the bush. Calvin and Brad give JJ a nod indicating they're all on the same page. Slowly they begin to peel back the shaking bush. The boys are apprehensive and curious at the same time as they move the bushes apart. With the bushes separated, the boys are caught by surprise when they find a young Hopi girl about the same age as them. She's dressed in a buckskin sleeveless dress and wears a gold medallion necklace, and around her wrist is a turquoise bracelet. Alongside her is a young Hopi boy about eleven years old. He is dressed in a buckskin breechcloth and has a bow with six arrows in a buckskin quiver over his shoulder. They slowly emerge from the bush and appear very frightened. The girl grasps the gold medallion necklace as if she feels should hide it from the strangers as she and the young boy somberly look up at JJ. JJ, sensing their trauma and confusion, gives them a gentle smile.

"Hello, my name is JJ, and these are my friends, Calvin and Brad," JJ says. Calvin smiles.

"Hi, I'm Calvin," replies Calvin. Brad leans forward and waves his hand.

"Yeah, don't mind us, we're just trying to get home," Brad says. The girl, slightly puzzled by Brad's hello, turns to JJ and smiles as the young boy squints his eyes and curiously scans the boys' clothing. JJ gives Inka a reassuring smile but feels he needs to explain who they are. He awkwardly proceeds.

"We're from a different time, but we saw the soldiers from the mountain and tried to get here in time to warn your village," JJ says. Inka gives JJ a puzzled look as if she doesn't quite understand what he meant when he said a different time. JJ frowns and continues.

"I'm sorry we were too late," JJ says with a somber face. Inka, appearing sad, lowers her head. JJ tries to comfort her and gives her a gentle pat on the back. She looks up at JJ with teary eyes.

"My father is the village chief; his name is Inkotoe," Inka

says. "He is the man the soldiers have taken to the post." Inka, looking despondent, blankly stares at the ground.

"I'm so scared, and I don't know where my mother is," Inka says. She lets loose of the gold medallion, covering her face with both hands, she starts to cry. Toeteeko gently reaches for his sister's arm. JJ sees a flash from the square gold medallion necklace and shares a glance with Calvin and Brad.

"So, if your father is the village chief, are you the village princess?" JJ asks.

"Yes," Inka responds. "My people call me Princess Inka." The boys share a curious look. JJ continues.

"Princess Inka, why have the soldiers come to your village?" JJ asks.

"I believe they have come looking for gold medallions," Inka replies.

"But why the gold medallions?" a curious JJ asks. Inka gives JJ a serious look. "Many years ago, as a boy, my father carved directions to a secret cave of Spanish treasure on two pieces of gold," Inka states as Calvin perks up and gets wide-eyed.

"A secret cave…where?" an excited Calvin asks. Inka points eastward.

"Somewhere hidden in the Mountains of the Morning Sun. When the two medallions are placed side-by-side, they reveal the directions to the cave," Inka says. Calvin gives JJ an "oh my gosh" look.

"Wow, she must mean the Superstition Mountains!" Calvin proclaims. The boys share curious expressions.

"So, the soldiers are looking for the two medallions?" JJ asks. Inka nods her head.

"Yes, my father wears one, and I wear the other," Inka states. The boys share a glance. Their eyebrows lower and they have serious faces as they realize the village is in greater danger than they thought. The boys are getting the sense things could get worse and most likely will. Inka sees the boys are looking apprehensive, so she decides to tell a family secret only two older village men know the story of. Inka gives the boys a soft smile.

"Please, let me tell you the story about the gold medallion maps," Inka offers.

The boys share a nod, then JJ, Calvin, Brad, and Toeteeko huddle close together with their eyes focused on Inka.

"Many years ago, my father was out hunting when a group of Spanish soldiers passed through our land," Inka begins. "He noticed two wagons filled with bags of gold coins and other treasures. When he noticed two square pieces of gold had fallen from the wagon, he decided to follow the soldiers," Inka continued. "He followed them all the way to the mountains and watched them carry the bags of gold to a cave. While hiding, he carved the direction on the two pieces of gold that had fallen from the wagon." The boys are mesmerized by the story and listen intently. Inka continues. "Just as he was done carving the directions, a young soldier sneaked up from behind him and wrapped his arm around my father's neck. They fought, and the only way for my father to escape was to use his knife. He had no choice and slashed the soldier's arm. The soldier lost his grip, and my father was freed but dropped the two gold medallion maps. The soldier noticed the gold maps had carvings and realized what my father had witnessed. So, when my father went to grab the maps, he also grabbed a handful of dirt. When he stood up, he was eye-to-eye with the young soldier, so he tossed the dirt into the soldier's eyes and ran away," Inka concludes her story and gives the boys a smile.

"Most of my tribe has gone north, but we have stayed to be the guardians of the secret cave and keepers of the medallion maps," Inka adds. The boys lean back and share a glance.

"Man, that was some story!" says Calvin. "Hey, JJ, do you think the Lost Dutchman's Mine is really the hidden Spanish gold in Inka's story?" JJ shrugs his shoulders.

"Could be, nobody has really ever found the Lost Dutchman's Mine," JJ says.

"Yeah, like…maybe they were a renegade group from Coronado's expedition!" an excited Calvin says.

"Who knows, but they were in these parts looking for the…Seven Cities of Cibola," JJ responds. "You know, the cities of gold." Suddenly a lance sails overhead, and the screams of desperation bring the boys back to reality. Inka gives the boys a hopeless look.

"JJ, I need your help, is there anything you and your friends can do?" a despondent Inka asks. JJ lips tighten, and inside he feels torn.

"Inka, I wish we could, but we got to figure out how to get home," JJ explains.

Inka brings her hands to her face and breaks down weeping. She looks at JJ with teary eyes, then covers her face, crying.

"I'm so afraid for my people," Inka says between tears. JJ tries to comfort Inka with a gentle pat on the shoulder. She looks up at JJ, and they share a smile. It's at this moment Inka and JJ share a special bond as if a destiny is unfolding.

JJ sports a serious expression and addresses Calvin and Brad.

"Look, guys, sometimes it's not what you want but what you give," JJ says.

Calvin nods his head and understands what JJ is saying. "Yeah, it's the right thing to do," Calvin says. Brad has a dubious look on his face. He stares off and shakes his head, then he gives JJ a stern look.

"Dudes, do we have time for this?" Brad asks in a concerned voice.

"I got a gut feeling. Something tells me we need to help Inka and her people," JJ responds. Brad looks to the ground, shaking his head. He looks up at JJ with a nod.

"Okay, then, so what's the plan?" Brad asks. JJ and Calvin flash smiles, and the boys share fist bumps.

Almost simultaneously in the center of the village, the conquistador captain intently stares at the gold medallion in his hand. He is in deep thought and looks curious.

"I must think…where have I seen those eyes?" the captain says in a frustrated tone.

As he looks down at the gold medallion, he sees the scar on his forearm. He gets wide-eyed, and at that moment, he realizes the village chief was the young Indian boy he fought at the site of the cave all those years ago. He perks up and flashes a serious face.

"Lieutenant, come here!" the captain yells.

The conquistador lieutenant with the black feather in his helmet rushes up to the captain. He salutes.

"Yes, Captain," says the lieutenant. The captain shows the lieutenant the gold medallion necklace.

"I'm going to tell you a story, Lieutenant," the captain says. "My captain fought with General Cortez, and after the fall of the Aztec Empire, he brought wagons of gold to this area and hide in the mountains. When we returned to New Spain, I became sick and had to stay behind when my captain and his men sailed to Cuba," the captain says as he stares off. "They all perished at sea during a storm leaving only me with knowledge of the secret cave of gold," the captain says. He sports a somber expression as he reflects on his past, then he flashes a serious face.

"Lieutenant, we have come to the right village, but this gold medallion necklace is only half of the map I'm looking for." His beady eyes scan the village. "Somewhere in this village is the other half," the captain proclaims as his eyes continue to search the village. He gives the lieutenant a menacing look.

"Lieutenant!" the captain shouts. The lieutenant snaps to attention.

"Yes, Captain?" says the lieutenant. The captain shows a mean expression as his face inches closer to the lieutenant.

"Do what you need to do to find the other necklace, do you understand, Lieutenant?" says the captain. "And, Lieutenant, I suggest you capture the chief's children to find the other half." The lieutenant nods his head.

"Yes, Captain," says the lieutenant. The captain gestures for the lieutenant to leave. He dashes away and signals for some soldiers to follow.

The conquistador captain mounts his horse and holds the gold medallion necklace high over his head. He then begins to trot his horse in a small circle to get his men's attention.

"Men!" the captain yells. "Somewhere in this village there's another gold medallion necklace like this one… whoever finds it will receive a bountiful award!" the captain announces. The soldiers salute the captain and scamper off to search the village for the other half of the gold medallion necklace.

Chapter Five

THE PLAN

JJ sports a serious face, and it's obvious he is deep in thought. Calvin, Brad, and JJ have committed to help Inka, so against overwhelming odds, he must figure out a way to accomplish this task. Time is critical as the group anxiously watches JJ, waiting for his plan. JJ rubs his chin and stares out toward the desert, then he hears a horse grunt. Close to the group near some bushes, a soldier's horse is freely standing alone and unguarded. The sound catches JJ's attention when suddenly as if a light bulb just went off, JJ perks up and flashes a confident smile.

"I got it!" says an excited JJ. "We'll divide, distract, and scare the soldiers so bad they'll never step foot on your land or village!" JJ proclaims.

Calvin and Brad share a confused glance while Inka and

Toeteeko appeared puzzled. Brad gives JJ a dubious grin.

"Sounds simple enough—WHAT?!" a bewildered Brad asks.

"Yeah, like how, JJ?" Inka asks. JJ hand gestures for the group to huddle up, then points to the lone horse.

"First, we divide. I'm going to use that horse to get the other horse soldiers to chase me, I know I can outride them and lose them in the desert," JJ says. He gives Calvin a serious look. "Calvin, do you got stuff in your backpack to build something that can fly?" JJ asks. Calvin pushes his glasses up off his nose and gives JJ a confident smirk of a smile.

"Me? Build something that can fly?" Calvin says, knowing the request is right up his alley. "Did the Wright brothers fly at Kitty Hawk?" Calvin asks in an "of course I can" manner.

JJ gives Calvin a smile and a fist bump.

"Great, but we got to act quick!" JJ says. "Calvin, what do you need from us to build the…" JJ ponders the name of the flying object as Calvin stares off wondering what he needs. Inka gets wide-eyed as if she has come up with a name.

"The War Bird!" Inka announces. "We'll call it the War Bird." The boys give Inka a smile.

"That's a good name, Inka. The War Bird it is," JJ says. Calvin looks at JJ as he picks up a stick.

"Here, this is what it will look like," Calvin says as he starts to draw in the desert ground and in a short time finishes his sketch. JJ and Brad share a glance.

"It's a Rembrandt," Brad sarcastically says. JJ shrugs his shoulders, then looks at Calvin.

"What's next?" JJ asks.

"Okay, this is what I need from you guys," Calvin says. "Some T-shirts to construct the wings." Calvin pauses and appears to be thinking as he rubs his chin.

"Okay, what else?" JJ asks. Calvin looks at Inka and Toeteeko.

"Toeteeko, I could use some of your arrows," Calvin says. Toeteeko grabs five arrows from his buckskin quiver.

"And, Inka, could you find me some wild berries?" Calvin asks. Inka smiles and nods her head as Calvin looks at Brad.

"Brad, I'll need you to find some long, straight branches to build the frame," Calvin adds.

Brad flashes a quick thumbs-up to Calvin.

"Ten-four, Kitty Hawk!" an eager Brad replies.

"Yep, we'll make one scary War Bird," Calvin says. "Plus, I've got a surprise for the captain."

"Sounds good, Calvin!" JJ responds. The boys are starting to feel confident they'll soon be able to help Inka and her people, but there's still some planning to figure out.

"Next, we need to free the village men," JJ says as he ponders how. Calvin stares off and appears to be in deep thought as he rubs his hands together. Suddenly Calvin gets wide-eyed and gives JJ an encouraging look.

"I know!" Calvin says. "Inka and I will disguise ourselves as a bush." The group curiously looks on and listens to Calvin's plan. "We'll sneak across to the cattle stockade and wait for the right time to free the men!" Calvin explains. Then he gives Inka a smile.

"Inka, once we get there, you can tell the men the plan," Calvin says. Inka smiles and is beginning to feel hopeful, so she nods her head in agreement.

"My people will be eager to help," Inka says. Calvin is thinking overtime and is on a roll. "Then when the scary War Bird is flying over the soldiers, the distraction will give us the chance to open the stockade fence!" an excited Calvin says to Inka. JJ is feeling Calvin's energy as the plan keeps unfolding. JJ gives Brad an encouraging look.

"Brad, the distraction will be the perfect chance to sneak up on the rock ledge to free Inka's father!" an enthusiastic JJ says. He looks at Toeteeko.

"Toeteeko, you go with Brad and cover his back." Toeteeko gives JJ a puzzled grin. "You know, his lookout," JJ explains. Toeteeko is eager to free his father, so he smiles and nods his head. The group feels confident. The boys fist bump, then show Inka and Toeteeko how to fist bump. No sooner than they share a laugh, a soldier is rustling through some nearby bushes. The group shares anxious glances as JJ places his finger on his lips.

"Shh," JJ quietly mutters as the group quickly crouches down to hide. The moment is tense as the soldier passes over their bush, but soon he leaves, and the group lets out a collective sigh. Inka gives the boys an encouraging but somber smile.

"You boys are so brave, you'll be heroes," Inka says. "I'll pray to the spirits to help you get home," she adds.

The boys are flattered by the compliment but realize the plan won't be easy. They give Inka a smile knowing they must fight through any apprehension and not let any doubt show on their faces. Then JJ and Inka catch eyes, and something deeper than a simple smile takes hold. They both have the same feeling, a special alliance, a bond, the feeling that they somehow have known each other. JJ is caught by surprise by these new feelings for Inka but realizes he must stay focused for survival is at stake.

"Come on, guys, let's get moving," JJ says. The group shares determined head nods, knowing they will need each other to overcome the odds to save Inka's father, the village, and the gold medallion necklaces.

The conquistador captain struggles to rally his soldiers as he gallops through the village trying to encourage his men while waving the gold medallion necklace high over his head. He is ruthless and determined and won't stop till he finds the other gold medallion necklace.

"Keep looking, men!" shouts the captain. "We must find the other half of the gold medallion necklace at all costs!" he demands. Then he gallops away on his horse and rides up to the rock ledge. He pulls the reins and stops in front of Chief Inkotoe, giving him a chilly eye.

"I know who you are now, and I know you remember me," says the captain. "Are you ready to tell me who has the other necklace, or do I need to find it the hard way—CHIEF?" the captain demands.

Chief Inkotoe squints his eyes and gives the captain a look of defiance.

"I will never tell you anything except leave my VIL-LAGE!" snaps the chief. The chief's strong voice rattles the horse, and the captain is taken aback by the chief's aggressive response. The captain pulls the reins to calm the animal and gives Chief Inkotoe a wry look. "So be it, Chief, have it your way," the captain says. He pulls the reins to the side and gallops away.

The War Bird, a colorful creation that resembles a vulture, lies on the desert ground. Calvin has positioned the solar panels on the back sides of the wings. Above the panels and attached to the body or frame is an airplane motor with the propeller in the reverse direction.

The reverse direction will push the bird forward, and with the motor at a slightly upward angle, the bird will always fly upward. The motor will be able to shift left to right to control turning. Calvin will adjust the power to fly up or down. String ties the T-shirts to the branches that make up the wings, and the branches are supported with Toeteeko's arrows. Duct tape holds the wings and frame together.

Berry juice on the T-shirts makes a pattern design to look like feathers, along with a pair of angry eyes near the beak. Tied inside the beak or mouth is one of the walkie-talkies. And palm leaves or fronds are scattered throughout the wings and frame with additional palm leaves making the rear tail.

The group is gathered, admiring the War Bird. Calvin and Inka are disguised as a bush with only their faces and the antenna from the remote-control panel exposed. JJ is on the horse securing the rope that hangs from the saddle horn as he gets ready. And Brad and Toeteeko stand ready for orders. Brad gives Calvin a big smile.

"Wow, Calvin, she's a beauty!" Brad says.

"Yeah, and I'm sure she's aerodynamically sound," Calvin replies. Brad nods this head.

"Cool, will it fly?" Brad asks. "Oh, and by the way, nice outfit!" he says with a chuckle. Calvin gives Brad a cynical look and shakes his head. JJ gives Calvin and Brad a serious look.

"Okay, guys, it's past noon, let's get this done," JJ says. Calvin suddenly sticks his arm through the bush waving his finger as he flashes a dubious face.

"There's just one thing," Calvin says in a hesitant manner. JJ sports a puzzled face and looks at Calvin.

"What's that?" JJ asks.

"I just realized the War Bird needs to be launched from a higher elevation," Calvin says in a tentative voice.

"Hmm…?" JJ mutters while looking puzzled.

"Yeah, kind of like a hang glider," Calvin responds. JJ nods his head and understands that the War Bird needs to be foot launched with plenty of air under the wings.

"I got it," JJ responds. Simultaneously JJ and Calvin both look at Brad. Brad looks around wondering what's going. Then his eyes suspiciously return to JJ and Calvin who are still looking at him.

"Why are you guys looking at me like that?" Brad asks. Calvin points to the tall rock formation directly behind where Chief Inkotoe is being held captive.

"That cliff above Chief Inkotoe," Calvin says. JJ gives a supportive head nod.

"Yeah, Brad, you're going to have to climb up the side of that rock formation," JJ adds.

Brad gives a suspicious look at the rock formation and rears his head, casting a dubious expression.

"Climb that…gigantic rock?!" Brad asks as he stares out toward the rock formation. JJ and Calvin continue to rally Brad on.

"Once you get to the top, you'll need to hoist the War Bird up to your location!" JJ says in an encouraging tone.

"The height will work perfect for the launch!" Calvin enthusiastically adds. Brad appears skeptical and rubs the back of his neck as his eyes scan the tall rock formation.

"Dudes, are you two sure about this?" Brad asks.

"Brad, you need to do this," JJ says. "Inka and Toeteeko are counting on you!" JJ adds.

Brad's face looks stolid as he lets out a long breath. He looks at Toeteeko who appears frightened and doleful. Brad knows if he doesn't launch the War Bird, the plan fails, and any hope of getting home could be lost. He looks at Toeteeko, then breaks a smile.

"Okay, now what's the plan again?" an eager Brad asks. The group tension starts to ease knowing that Brad is on board with the launch requirements. Calvin gives Brad a smile.

"Wait for my signal before you launch the bird, and remember, you'll need to let JJ know you're launching," Calvin says.

"Yeah, once I get your signal, I can start the War Bird screams," JJ says. Calvin gives Brad an anxious look.

"And don't forget to turn on the walkie-talkie power button!" Calvin includes. Brad gets a little defensive but realizes this is a lot of information for him to digest.

"I'm not going to forget, geez!" Brad says. "Then what?" he asks.

"Once you give me the signal, the screaming War Bird will distract the soldiers. That's when you climb down the rope and free Inka's father," JJ explains. Brad flashes a bewildered expression and takes a hard look at the steep cliff in the front of the rock formation.

"Climb down the rope?" Brad mutters out loud.

"I'll ride up with the horse and get Chief Inkotoe," says a confident JJ. "It's a great plan!" proclaims JJ.

"Then at the right moment, I'll give the conquistador captain his big surprise and—POW—out goes the lights!" an excited Calvin adds.

Inka and Toeteeko share a hopeful smile and are feeling better among all the despair knowing that the boys are determined to help. JJ and Calvin are feeling confident they have come up with a good plan. Brad on the other hand is a bit skeptical but would never let his friends down. The group is ready and soon will be on the move.

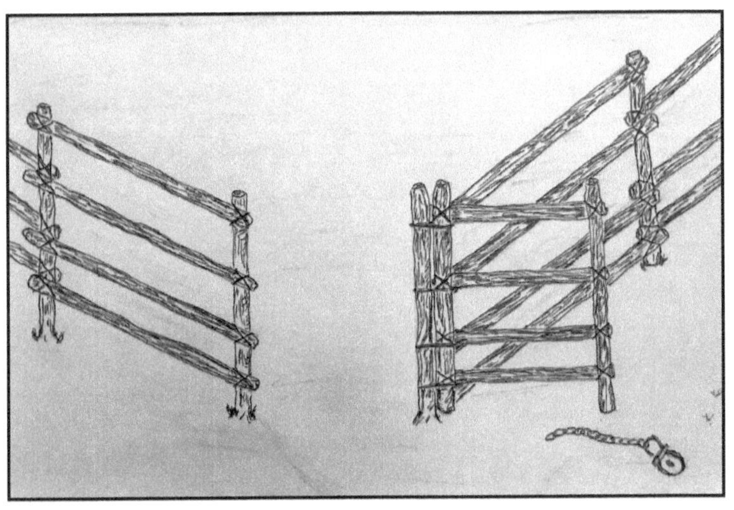

Chapter Six

SAVING THE VILLAGE

Chief Inkotoe remains tied to the wooden post. Under the hot desert sun, he is beginning to frail as his head droops side to side. He is starting to feel all is lost. His men have been rounded up and held captive in the cattle stockade. There is no one left who can fight the invaders, and he's becoming weaker and weaker by the moment. The feeling of helplessness has dashed any signs of hope. He lifts his head and looks toward the village, then looks up to the sky.

"Father in the heavens, please give me the strength to help my people," a weak Chief Inkotoe mutters. His eyes close as anguish and pain fill his face. He drops his head.

The group is prepared to execute their plan. JJ has mounted the horse and is crouched over to avoid being seen. Calvin and Inka are disguised as a bush and well camouflaged. Brad and Toeteeko are holding the War Bird and ready to move out. Through the bush, Calvin hands Brad a large rock and his backpack.

"Here's the surprise for that captain," Calvin says. "Jam this rock between the landing gear and I'll release it from the remote control!" an enthusiastic Calvin says. Brad perks up and flashes a big smile.

"Cool," Brad replies. JJ flashes a big smile and gives the group a thumbs-up.

"Good luck, guys!" JJ says as he pulls the reins and gets the horse's attention.

"Giddyup!" commands JJ. He takes off with a hard gallop as the group watches JJ charging toward the center of the village, leaving a trail of dust behind him.

The conquistador captain, his lieutenant, and four horse soldiers are gathered in the center of the village. Suddenly JJ blasts right past them without any hesitation. The group of conquistadors are caught off guard and look surprised as their eyes follow JJ. The conquistador captain shakes his head in disbelief, then realizing what's going on, he flashes an angry face.

"Get him!" the captain yells.

The lieutenant and the four horse soldiers share confused glances. Then the lieutenant pounds his boots into the horse's side and takes off after JJ. The four horse soldiers quickly follow.

JJ has charged through the center of the village and has reached the desert. JJ's legs press the horse to gallop faster.

"Hyah, hyah!" JJ calls out to the horse. "Let's go, boys, hyah!" JJ takes a quick look behind him, then pounds his hat against the animal's hind leg. The horse picks up the gallop.

"Yeah, they've taken the bait!" JJ enthusiastically says.

JJ doesn't work a horse this hard, but this is the race of his life. He has no other option but to get everything he can out of the animal.

In hot pursuit and close behind him, the conquistador lieutenant leads the four horse soldiers in the chase. The pounding of horse hooves rumbles through the desert as JJ with unyielding determination leads the conquistador soldiers farther out into the desert with each swift gallop.

Suddenly a lance zips through the air and barely misses JJ. He takes a quick peek at the horse soldiers, then aggressively pushes forward.

"Hyah, Hyah!" JJ yells. But the horse soldiers are slowly gaining, and the lance was dangerously too close. He realizes he must do something quick or else. So JJ does what JJ can do great, and he breaks into spectacular horse-riding maneuvers. Without hesitation he positions himself on one side of the horse and then kicks his boot into the ground, whipping himself to the other side.

The whoosh of a lance echoes in JJ's ear. Then he quickly rides underneath the horse while in full gallop, taking the target from the soldiers. Almost immediately he's back in the saddle, pounding his hat against the horse's back leg.

JJ takes a quick look at the soldiers, and it's obvious the chase is tight, and the soldiers are skilled horsemen riding powerful animals.

"You're doing great, boy!" JJ says. "Hyah, Hyah!" he yells. "Dig it in!"

Ahead of JJ is a desert full of large sequoia cacti and an opportunity to slow the horse soldiers. He begins to zigzag between the cacti, much as if he was practicing at home with barrels. Another lance pierces the air just missing JJ and slamming into a cactus, penetrating the giant plant. He takes a quick peek at the soldiers.

"These guys are good!" JJ proclaims as he looks for obstacles to slow the soldiers. Then he suddenly gets wide-eyed and flashes a mischievous smile.

"Perfect…a river," JJ says. "I've got them now."

A lance whooshes past JJ as his leg presses the horse to keep the strong gallop. JJ sports a slight smile knowing this is the opportunity he needs for the advantage to be on his side.

In the foreground, a river about twenty yards wide flows with a strong current. The river takes a sharp right bend with a fifteen-foot-high bank on JJ's side and flat river rock on the other side.

The horse keeps the strong gallop as JJ waves his hat in the air, taunting the soldiers who are only about twenty yards behind JJ. The conquistador lieutenant and the horse soldiers relentlessly continue their chase. Little by little they have been closing in and feel confident they'll run down the troublemaker. A lance whooshes and zings past JJ as he pounds horse hooves and pushes hard to get to the river.

JJ is working the animal hard. He leans forward close to the horse's ear.

"Okay, big guy, trust me, I know you can do this," JJ says. He takes a quick glance at the soldiers, then with fixed eyes, he stares down the river knowing the advantage is on his side. His calculation is simple, and he is betting on his life he is correct.

"With all that heavy gear, they'll never make this jump," says JJ as the river approaches at a quick, tense pace. In his mind he knows an error will spell disaster or worse. JJ looks determined the final split second.

"Jump!" JJ yells. The horse follows the command and makes its jump at the prefect spot. The animal gracefully sails over the river. JJ waves his hat in midair as he makes the daring jump over the strong currents.

"Hy-aah!" JJ shouts in his best cowboy cry. They come down hard on the flat river rock but have made the jump. JJ's ecstatic and proud of the horse he had faith in.

"That a boy, you did it!" JJ says as he rubs the horse's neck. He looks across the river toward the oncoming soldiers. Led by the conquistador lieutenant, they hit the high bank and make the jump. But JJ's gamble has paid off as one-by-one they follow their lieutenant and splash land into the middle of the river.

Panic covers their faces as they're swept downstream. The unlucky ones go under from the weight of their armor as the rest vanish out of sight. JJ nods his head and continues to pet the horse's neck as he watches the last soldiers disappear.

"Divide and conquer," a somber JJ says. "Okay, boy, let's find a place to cross and wait for the signal, giddyup." He gives the reins a slight tug, and the horse trots away.

The bush is positioned by the stockade fence. The soldiers, and even the men held captive, are unaware of the clever disguise. Calvin and Inka peek their heads out from the bush and curiously check out the surroundings. They cautiously watch a soldier walk up to the fence gate where he uses a key to release a padlock and adjusts the chain that holds the gate to a fence post. These objects and devices are new to Inka, and she studies the soldier's every move. All seems to be going well until Calvin looks toward the ground and sees a large black scorpion crawling toward the bush. Calvin cringes as panic covers his face. His eyebrows lower, and his lips tighten as he tries to fight the fear. Calvin knows if he panics, he'll give away the disguise, and the consequences could be dismal. Then his moment of truth, Calvin shakes his head and flashes a look of determination.

"It's time to Eagle Scout down!" Calvin quietly proclaims, and he looks at Inka.

"Inka, we made it, tell the men the plan," Calvin says. Inka flashes a confident smile.

"Okay," Inka responds. She looks toward the stockade and gets wide-eyed as she sees an old family friend.

"Psst, Toemeeka!" Inka quietly calls out. She hands gestures for her friend to come over.

Toemeeka is a village man who was like Chief Inkotoe's younger brother when they were growing up together in the village. He is happy but surprised to see Inka. "Princess Inka, it's good to see you're safe!" Toemeeka says. "We heard you and Toeteeko did not escape with your mother." Princess Inka smiles and is much relieved by the news her mother is safe.

"Oh, thanks the heavens!" an exuberant Inka says. Toemeeka gives Princess Inka a serious look.

"Princess Inka, you are not safe here, you must leave!" Toemeeka says, obviously very concerned for Princess Inka's safety. Inka gives him a stout look.

"Toemeeka, I could never leave my people and our village!" Inka responds with strong conviction. Inka begins to realize that she needs to provide courage and be a leader of her people while her father is held captive. She gives Toemeeka a hopeful smile and gestures for him to get closer.

"Listen, we have a plan and tell the men to be ready," Inka announces. Toemeeka's eyes light up, and for the first time, he feels hope and encouragement. He nods his head and leans over to listen.

Brad and Toeteeko are holding the War Brid as Brad looks up the side of the steep rock formation. He appears dubious as he shakes his head and flashes a cringe.

"You're kidding me!" Brad grumbles out loud. Toeteeko gives Brad a puzzled look and wonders what Brad is saying.

"What is it?" Toeteeko curiously asks. Brad realizes he has somewhat alarmed Toeteeko and knows he needs to stay calm. Brad gives Toeteeko a reassuring smile.

"Oh, aah…nothing," Brad replies. "Look, let your father know we're here."

Toeteeko smiles and gives a head nod. He cups his hands around his mouth and makes a sound like a cricket—CHIC, CHIC—then he pauses for a second and repeats the sound.

Chief Inkotoe lifts his head and looks toward the bushes.

He knows the sound came from his son, a sound Toeteeko has made while playing since he was a young child. He smiles and lowers his weary head. Brad and Toeteeko share a smile as Brad flashes a thumbs-up.

"That was cool," Brad says. "Well, I guess I better get ready, keep me covered." Brad cautiously steps out from behind some bushes and positions himself near the base of the rock formation and begins to make his climb. The rope is tied to his waist and the other end to the front of the War Bird. Brad slowly edges himself up the steep rock formation and has wisely picked a spot out of view of the soldiers in the village. He struggles but steadily advances upward as the slack in the rope begins to tighten. Brad looks up the side of the rock and then down toward the ground.

"Wow, this cliff is higher than it looks," Brad mutters to himself as he continues to press upward.

It's later, and Brad is about halfway up the side of the rock formation. He carefully places one hand after another on the rock ledge and pulls himself up. Brad struggles with the climb but knows he needs to complete his mission.

"Don't look down, just don't look down," an anxious Brad mutters to himself. Brad slowly pulls his head above a rock ledge when he becomes eye-to-eye with a coiled rattlesnake. The rattle of the snake's tail chills the air as the snake slowly rears its head back to strike. Brad gets bug-eyed and is frozen in fear at the sight of the snake. It's a hopeless situation.

"Yikes!" Brad yells. He knows he's doomed, and he only has two options, either he jumps and suffers from the fall or it's the snake bite. The snake rears its head another couple more inches as the forked tongue whips around. The snake's beady eyes are focused on Brad. Then suddenly the swoosh of an arrow strikes the snake, knocking off the cliff ledge.

Brad lets out a big sigh of relief and looks down toward Toeteeko who is holding his bow. Brad gives Toeteeko a thumbs-up, and he returns the gesture with a proud grin. Brad knows Toeteeko just saved his life and is even more motivated to complete the climb.

"That was close," Brad says. "Almost there."

Chief Inkotoe remains tied to the post and his head droops down. He is weak and feeling helpless for his people. Suddenly off to the side of a roll of bushes, Toeteeko's face appears. He quickly scans the area, then cautiously leaves the bushes and sneaks up onto the ledge. He crawls to his father while making sure he is not seen.

"Father," Toeteeko says. Chief Inkotoe opens a weary eye and looks down to Toeteeko with a smile. "We have friends who are helping us. Our people will be free soon!" Toeteeko announces. He pulls out his hunting knife and starts to cut the ropes at his father's ankle. Chief Inkotoe, although feeling weak, nods his head acknowledging his son. As Toeteeko cuts the rope, Chief Inkotoe looks toward the other end of the long ledge and suddenly get wide-eyed.

"Toeteeko, quick, you must hide!" an anxious Inkotoe says. "They're two soldiers coming!"

Two conquistador soldiers dressed in full heavy armor are marching toward Chief Inkotoe to serve as guards. Each soldier carries a spear plus a sword and knife attached to a belt. Toeteeko sees the two soldiers and quickly crawls off the ledge. He scampers to the bushes and hides.

Meanwhile, Brad is pushing forward with his climb when suddenly his foot slips, and he finds himself dangling on the steep rock wall while holding on with one hand. Small rocks rumble to the ground, but fortunately for Brad, the noise doesn't attract any attention. Brad struggles to get a grip, and eventually he is able to secure himself from the mishap and continue his climb. Moments later Brad has reached the top and finishes his climb. He looks over the ledge and shakes his head.

"Wow, that's a long way down there," Brad says as he searches for Toeteeko.

"Toeteeko?" Brad wonders where Toeteeko has gone as he starts to pull the rope up to hoist the War Bird to the top. Brad is positioned near the edge and out of view but is unable to see Chief Inkotoe from his vantage point.

Calvin's and Inka's faces are outside the bush. Calvin is holding the remote-control panel and waits for his signal. Calvin's eyes search for some clue from Brad when suddenly a look of panic covers his face.

"Oh no!" Calvin says. "This isn't good." Inka senses Calvin's concern but doesn't quite understand what's going on.

"What is it?" Inka asks.

"Geez, two soldiers are guarding your father, and I don't think Brad knows!" an antsy Calvin responds. Inka gives Calvin a puzzled expression.

"What's he going to do?" asks a concerned Inka.

"I don't know…I need to warn him before he launches the War Bird… Man, I got to tell, JJ!" a desperate Calvin says as he nervously operates the walkie-talkie.

"Hey, Brad, can you read me?" Calvin asks. "Nothing… Come in, Brad!" Calvin shakes his head realizing he's not getting through to Brad. Calvin stares out toward the desert.

"JJ, can you read me?" Calvin asks.

JJ is looking very concerned as he operates the walkie-talkie. He's crouched over in the saddle behind some bushes to keep his cover.

"Calvin, what's going on!" an anxious JJ asks.

"I see two guards by Chief Inkotoe, they weren't in the plan!" JJ listens intently for Calvin's reply. Both boys know the entire operation is in jeopardy. There's a slight crackle from the walkie-talkie, then Calvin's voice.

"Are you thinking…what I'm thinking?" a nervous Calvin asks. At that moment both boys realize the same thing at the same time and simultaneously react.

"He forgot to turn the power button…ON!" JJ and Calvin say together. JJ closes his eyes and just shakes his head. He stares out toward the rock formation hoping for the best. Then he lifts the walkie-talkie to his mouth.

"Calvin, he's got to launch the War Bird, or we don't have a chance," JJ says.

Calvin frantically is working the walkie-talkie. He knows the element of surprise will be lost if Brad doesn't launch the War Bird soon. Inka anxiously watches Calvin.

"I know, I know…I'll keep trying," Calvin says to JJ. "Hey, Brad…Brad, it's time to launch the War Bird…I repeat!" a desperate Calvin says.

Brad is kneeling at the top of the cliff but out of sight to anyone. He's holding the War Bird and is anxious to launch but remains unaware of the two guards.

"Any moment now I should get the signal, and this baby is taking off," Brads says to himself. He leans over and peeks out toward the village but not at enough of an angle to look down. He rubs the back of his neck and looks puzzled.

"Hmm…that's strange, why haven't I heard from Calvin?" Brad mutters as he stares off thinking about his part of the plan.

"Am I forgetting something?" Brad squints his eyes and tries to think as hard as he can. He looks at the rock jammed between the landing gear, then looks at the walkie-talkie tied to the beak. A close look at the walkie-talkie reveals the volume button is on high, but the power button is in the off position. Brad gets wide-eyed and realizes what he forgot.

"Oops," Brad says. "I forgot to turn the power on." He reaches down to turn on the power button.

At the same time Brad is reaching for the power button, Calvin is looking nervous and dripping sweat. He has reached the tipping point of desperation, knowing the plan is about to go down the drain.

"Brad, please come in!" Calvin says. "If you can hear me, there's two soldiers guarding Chief Inkotoe, but it's time to launch the War Bird!" an exhausted Calvin says.

But just at that exact moment Brad has turn on the power button, and all he hears is, "launch the War Bird." Brad gets wide-eyed and is pumped up after hearing his clue.

"Well, it's about time, Calvin!" an excited Brad says. He stands up and takes a couple of steps back, then leans forward as close as he can get to the walkie-talkie. He pushes the talk button.

"JJ, it's launch time!" an exuberant Brad announces. He holds the War Bird over his head, and with three quick steps forward, he launches the War Bird with a mighty heave, and off the War Bird goes, sailing away from the steep rock formation and heading toward the center of the village just as planned, except Brad is still unaware of the guards.

JJ in desperation tries to warn Brad one more time about the two guards.

"Hey, Brad, there's two guards…," JJ says as he realizes it's too late and watches the War Bird take flight.

Back at the stockade Calvin and Inka see the War Bird is airborne, and the plan is in motion. Calvin is much relieved and sports a determined look as he methodically operates the remote-control panel.

"Okay, here we go!" Calvin says.

The War Bird has successfully taken flight, and with Calvin in control, the War Bird is flying large circular patterns over the soldiers. To get the soldiers' attention, Calvin has the War Bird swooping up and down over the soldiers. They appear startled and puzzled at the sight of such a large bird.

Back in the desert, JJ is charging full gallop toward the village, leaving behind a trail of dust. He brings the walkie-talkie to his mouth and begins the bird's war cries.

"Hawk, hawk…caw, caw!" JJ screams into the walkie-talkie.

The conquistador captain's horse is restless, and he is surrounded by frightened soldiers as the screaming War Bird swoops down upon his men. A petrified soldier looks up to his captain.

"Captain, what is this huge bird?" the frightened soldier asks. The captain realizes he must keep his men calm and focused on finding the other half of the gold medallion necklace.

"Do not be frightened, men, it's nothing but a large vulture!" the captain replies as he struggles to keep his horse from panicking.

JJ is pressing his horse to a fast gallop while screaming into the walkie-talkie. Then JJ realizes to really scare the soldiers and get all their attention, he needs to put fear into their hearts. So JJ decides to speak Spanish to the soldiers.

"Conquistadores españoles, deje este pueblo antes de que morderte la cabeza!" JJ yells into the walkie-talkie.

Back at the stockade, Calvin and Inka remain hiding in the

bush as he continues to operate the remote control. Calvin, who knows how to speak several languages, hears what JJ has just said and is taken by surprise by the words.

"Oh, nice, JJ!" Calvin says. Inka appears curious and looks at Calvin.

"Calvin, what's JJ saying?" Inka asks. Calvin gives Inka a cringed expression.

"He's telling the soldiers he's going to bite their heads off," Calvin replies. Inka flashes a squeamish look.

In center of the village, the captain and the soldiers are watching the War Bird with fixed eyes. JJ's screams are starting to take its toll as fear starts to turn into panic. The captain tries his best to calm his men.

"Soldiers, don't be frightened, it's just a large bird that's… talking to us!" the desperate captain says.

The two soldiers guarding Chief Inkotoe are standing near the edge of the ledge. They're hunched over clutching their lances with the look of horror in their eyes. Then behind the soldiers, a rope descends from the cliff, and shortly after that, Brad is climbing down the rope as planned.

"Don't look down, just don't look down," an apprehensive Brad mutters to himself while totally unaware of the two guards.

Back in the desert, JJ gets wide-eyed as he sees Brad climbing down the rope. He knows Brad is in big trouble, and he must keep the soldier's attention on the War Bird. JJ readies the walkie-talkie.

"Sodados invasores, deja esta tierra antes de que les saque los ojos!" JJ screams into the walkie-talkie.

Calvin and Inka remain hidden in the bush waiting for the moment to let the men out. Calvin hears what JJ has just screamed out. His face cringes, and his jaw drops in disgust.

"Ugh, JJ, come on, man!" Calvin cries out. Inka sees the face on Calvin and is more than curious to know what JJ said.

"What did he say?" Inka asks. "What's he saying now?" Calvin turns to Inka sporting a face like he just stepped into something gross.

"He told the invading soldiers to leave this land before I pick their eyes out!" Calvin responds with a sour face.

The conquistador captain's horse is almost uncontrollable; the animal is up on its hind legs and making horse grunting sounds. The soldiers are in panic mode. They're covering their eyes and running in all directions.

The War Bird is doing what the boys had planned on. Calvin has the bird swooping up and down in a relentless fashion. JJ's timing with the screaming bird is spot-on. Just as the War Bird swoops down JJ lets out another repulsive message.

"Deja esta tierra antes de que te arranque las lenguas y darles de comer a las hormigas!" flies out from the War Bird.

Calvin just shakes his head after hearing JJ's line and is taken aback by the savageness of his words.

"No…JJ!" Calvin says with a cringe. "Leave this land before I rip your tongues out and feed them to the ants!" Calvin and Inka share a horrid glance.

"Yuck!" they say together.

At the steep rock formation, Brad continues to climb down the rope, and with all the commotion, he is still unaware of the two guards. Fortunately for Brad at this point all eyes are fixed on the War Bird.

Brad peeks down to the ledge's surface and feels it's safe enough to let go of the rope and drop to the ledge.

"Great, close enough, I'm jumping from here," Brad says. He lets go of the rope, and within a split second, he lands feetfirst smacking onto the ledge. But the noise doesn't go unnoticed. Immediately the two guards and Chief Inkotoe look toward Brad.

The first soldier, the one closest to Brad, readies his spear and rushes toward Brad. Brad is just straightening up after the jump and turns around. An unsuspecting Brad for the first time sees the two soldiers guarding Chief Inkotoe.

"Whoa!" a surprised Brad says. "Where did you guys come from?" And almost simultaneously the guard tosses the spear, then quickly draws his sword. The spear zips through the air and is sailing right at Brad's head. He dodges the spear as it passes under Brad's chin, crashing into the side of the rock formation.

"Dude!" Brad shouts. He realizes he must rely on his karate training and knows he must fight one guard at a time. Brad is apprehensive and worried but knows the fight is on. So he makes a move to his right, knowing he must position himself away from the second guard so he can concentrate on the first guard. Brad readies himself into a martial arts fighting posture as the guard rushes toward him violently swinging his sword back and forth.

"Arghh!" the guard growls out as he closes in on Brad. Within a second Brad finds himself toe-to-toe with the angry guard and the blade of the sword. He ducks, bobs, and weaves to avoid the sharp edges of steel. The swish of the blade hums in Brad's ear with each pass.

The guard raises the sword high over his head and lunges toward Brad. Brad sees an opportunity and seizes it. He grabs the guard's arm and conducts a perfect judo flip, sending the guard over Brad's upper body and slamming him onto the ledge's surface. The guard cringes in pain, taken aback by such a defensive move. The guard staggers to his feet and looks determined to carry out the fight. Brad feels confident and readies himself into a fighting position.

"Here's my newest move, dude!" Brad says. Then he executes a flawless right leg reverse-crescent kick and delivers a decisive striking blow to the guard's right jaw. The guard's knees buckle as he staggers and falls off the ledge. Brad takes a quick peek over the ledge's edge.

"One down and one to go," Brad quietly says. Suddenly Toeteeko, who is now standing behind the second guard, notices Brad is in immediate danger.

"Brad, look out!" Toeteeko screams out in terror as the second guard hurls his spear directly at Brad's back. Toeteeko's warning has given Brad the time to react. He quickly turns around and uses his forearm to block and deflect the spear.

"Thanks, little buddy!" Brad says.

The guard turns around and sees Toeteeko. He immediately grabs the young Indian boy by the arm and pulls his sword out, placing the edge on Toeteeko's throat. Chief Inkotoe squints his eyes in horror as he watches the danger his only son is in.

Brad knows he must coerce the guard into a fight and away from Toeteeko. His eyebrows lower, and with fixed eyes on his opponent, a determined Brad stares down the guard.

"Okay, Mr. Tough Guy…how about you and me?" Brad says as he walks closer to the guard while tapping his chest. Brad is doing his best to egg on the guard when suddenly the guard could no longer resist. He slams Toeteeko to the ground and walks toward Brad with sword in hand.

"Yes, I need to take care of you before I deal with these two," the angry guard says.

Quietly, Toeteeko pulls out his hunting knife and crawls toward the rope around his father's ankles. At the same moment, Brad squares off in his fighting position in front of the guard. The guard quickly lunges at Brad while swinging his sword. The zing of the blade cuts through the air as Brad bobs and weaves, avoiding the steel. Then Brad ducks and simultaneously conducts a leg sweep that efficiently drops the guard to the ledge's surface and dislodges the sword from his hand.

"Ugh!" the guard grunts out as the sword crashes to the ground. Brad again seizes the opportunity and kicks the sword off the ledge with his shoe. The guard helplessly watches the sword fall out of sight, but he is not finished. He gets up and pulls a knife, then jabs the blade directly in front of him as he advances toward Brad. He sees another opportunity, with the knife in front, it's exposed, and Brad knows exactly what to do. He immediately conducts a right leg crescent kick, knocking the knife out of the guard's hand. The guard is startled as he watches the knife sail out of reach. Brad gets back into his fighting position, but then he cracks a smile and nods his head as if he just realized something. Then the smile leaves, and he looks at the guard with laser eyes.

"Own the moment…I get it," Brad says to himself as he gets into his martial arts fighting position. With a blink of an eye, he jumps straight up and performs a 360-degree right-foot roundhouse kick aimed directly at the guard's left jaw. Brad's gym shoe slams into the guard's jaw, making him stagger backward. Then Brad quickly employs a series of powerful front karate kicks into the guard's armored chest, driving him farther backward.

At the same time Brad is driving the guard backward with karate kicks, Toeteeko has just finished cutting his father's ankles free. Chief Inkotoe and Toeteeko share a smile as Brad continues his relentless karate kicks. The guard staggers in front of Chief Inkotoe who lifts both legs and gives the guard one final kick, knocking him off the ledge. Brad and Chief Inkotoe share a smile, then Brad walks over to the ledge's edge and looks down to see the two guards lying on the ground. Brad lets out a big sigh of relief thinking the fight is over when he is suddenly slammed to the ground. Brad is shaken and startled for out of nowhere, completely unnoticed, a soldier is standing over him with a knife in his hand. The soldier immediately jumps on Brad and grabs his right arm while thrusting the knife toward Brad's throat. Brad grabs the soldier's wrist and pushes back. Brad and the soldier are face-to-face as the knife inches closer and closer to his throat.

Chief Inkotoe looks on in horror and anxiously stares down at Toeteeko who is frantically cutting away at the ropes that bind his father's hands. Suddenly the rope falls free, and without hesitation Chief Inkotoe dashes to help Brad in his struggle. The situation is dire for Brad, when Chief Inkotoe in the nick of time grabs the soldier's wrist that is holding the knife and pushes his arm up and the knife away from Brad's throat. With the soldier's side exposed, Chief Inkotoe uses his right foot and pushes the soldier off Brad.

The soldier and Brad both jump to their feet and prepare for battle. Standing to Brad's left and slightly behind him, Chief Inkotoe and Toeteeko anxiously watch. The soldier gives Brad a mean-looking stare as he gets ready to throw the knife at Brad. Then the soldier looks at Chief Inkotoe and suddenly throws the knife at him. The knife sails through the air, tumbling in motion and traveling straight toward Chief Inkotoe's chest. He looks terrified and frozen in fear as Toeteeko looks on in shock.

"Father!" Toeteeko screams. Brad only has a split second to react. He sees the knife tumbling right at Chief Inkotoe's chest and rapidly conducts a reverse right leg roundhouse kick, knocking the knife to the ledge's surface.

Brad quickly gets into his martial arts position and readies himself for combat.

"Own the moment…part two," Brad says. Then he

takes one step forward and jumps straight up, conducting a frontal karate kick delivering a decisive blow to the soldier's face. He staggers and falls off the ledge.

Chief Inkotoe and Toeteeko rush up to Brad.

"Brad, you saved my father!" a jubilant Toeteeko says. Brad gives Toeteeko a smile.

"We saved each other," Brad responds as Chief Inkotoe flashes a proud grin.

"Great fighting brave warrior!" Chief says. He looks down to Toeteeko and flashes a worried expression.

"Toeteeko, where is Inka?" a concerned Chief Inkotoe asks about his daughter. Toeteeko flashes a big smile.

"Father, Brad and his friends have a plan to save the village!" an excited Toeteeko announces.

"A plan?" Chief Inkotoe curiously asks. Brad gives Chief Inkotoe an encouraging look.

"Yes, sir, Inka is with my friend Calvin, and they're ready to free the men so you can lead them against the soldiers," Brad explains.

JJ suddenly gallops up to the group. He's about shoulder high to the ledge.

"Brad, that was awesome!" an excited JJ says.

"Father, this is Inka's friend, JJ," Toeteeko says while JJ tips his cowboy hat.

"Pleasure to meet you, Chief Inkotoe," JJ says. Then JJ gives Chief Inkotoe a serious look and appears anxious.

"Chief Inkotoe, I need to take you to Inka so you can

lead the men, quick, get on!" JJ strongly suggests. And without any hesitation, Chief Inkotoe gets on the horse with JJ as Brad and Toeteeko watch. Chief Inkotoe gives his son a concerned look.

"Toeteeko, take Brad with you and find your mother. I'm worried about her safety!" a concerned Inkotoe tells his son.

"Yes, father," Toeteeko replies. JJ tugs the reins, and they fast gallop to the stockade.

Calvin and Inka remain hidden in the bush as Calvin continues to negotiate the War Bird. In the background a couple of dozen village men watch the action and anxiously wait for the signal.

"Inka, they did it!" Calvin enthusiastically announces. "Your father is free; now is the time to unlock the gate!" Inka flashes a big smile and quickly gets out of the bush. She picks up a lance lying on the ground and rushes to the stockade gate. Then very wisely she jams the lance tip into the lock and uses it like a key.

"I'll keep the captain and the soldiers busy," Calvin says as Inka works on the lock.

The War Bird is flying circles over the soldiers. They look

frightened, and some are crouched in fear as others jab their lances in the sky as the bird calls out its screams. The captain struggles to keep his horse under control and his men disciplined. He aggressively swings his sword and desperately tries to rally his men.

"Don't be frightened, remember, we need to find the other half of the gold medallion necklace, and we'll all be rich!" the captain proclaims.

JJ and Chief Inkotoe gallop up to the stockade fence. Inka is standing next to the open gate with the lance in her hand. The village men pump their fists in the air and celebrate at the sight of the chief. They quickly rush to their leader and enthusiastically surround him.

Chief Inkotoe leans over and gives Inka a hug, they separate, and she gives the lance to her father.

"Inka, your warriors' plan is about to work!" Chief Inkotoe announces. He looks at the village men and raises the lance over his head.

"We will attack from three directions and surround the invaders. Toemeeka, you take a group and attack from the right flank. Inka, you take another group and attack from the left flank. I'll take the third group to attack the center and find the conquistador captain," a defiant Chief Inkotoe orders.

"Let us fight hard and take back our village!" Chief Inkotoe declares. The village men break out in a loud cheer and look ready for a fight. JJ and Chief Inkotoe gallop away, followed by a group of village men, then burst into a charge toward the center of the soldiers. The other men enthusiastically follow Toemeeka and Inka.

Calvin is busy with the remote control. He flashes a devious smile.

"It's time for the captain's surprise," Calvin mutters to himself.

In the center of the village, Chief Inkotoe and the village men battle the soldiers. The conquistador captain wildly swings his sword and rallies his men in battle.

"Keep fighting, men, we must find the other gold medallion necklace!" the captain yells out. Suddenly the War Bird swoops down on the captain, barely missing his head. Just as Calvin planned, the bird got his attention. The captain watches the bird fly upward and conduct an aerial turnaround loop, then like a dive bomber, the War Bird goes straight for the captain. The captain watches the War Bird and gets wide-eyed when he sees the huge bird is not flying away but heading right at him.

Calvin is aggressively managing the remote control with a devilish smile as he looks out toward the center of the village.

"Wheels up," Calvin says.

The War Bird is streaking right for the conquistador captain when the landing gears pull up, releasing the rock. The rock falls straight toward the captain as the bird pulls out of the dive. The captain is beside himself, and before he can react, he is smacked with the rock right on his helmet. He is knocked off his horse and falls to the ground unconscious.

Calvin flashes a big grin while nodding his head.

"Bull's-eye, who's your daddy!" a triumphant Calvin announces.

JJ and Chief Inkotoe immediately ride up to the captain who's semi-unconscious on his back, holding his helmet and moaning in pain. Chief Inkotoe dismounts from the horse and walks up to the conquistador captain.

"Get him!" Chief Inkotoe orders. Two village men pick the captain up off the ground by his arms. His head droops forward, rolling back and forth. Chief Inkotoe gives the captain a serious look, then looks out toward the fighting.

"Soldiers!" Chief Inkotoe calls out. "If you ever want to see your captain again, drop your weapons and leave our village…or else the sacred War Bird will haunt you forever!"

The soldiers and the village men stop fighting. The soldiers see their captain is finished, so they drop their swords and lances to the ground. Soon a horse-drawn wagon rolls up next to the captain as the two village men hand over the captain to two soldiers. Chief Inkotoe looks on, then suddenly flashes a serious expression.

"Wait!" Chief Inkotoe says. He walks up to the captain and grabs his hand that clutches the gold medallion necklace.

"You have something that is ours," Chief Inkotoe calls out. He rips the medallion out of the captain's hand, then gives the soldiers an evil eye.

"Go!" Chief Inkotoe demands. The soldiers quickly place the defeated conquistador captain in the back of the wagon, and within a moment's time, the wagon wheels turn as they head out of the village followed by the soldiers.

Inka runs up to her father, followed by Toeteeko and her mother. Brad is standing next to JJ, who is still on the horse, and Calvin, who is still disguised as a bush, joins the group.

"Father, I was so frightened, but my friends have saved our village!" a jubilant Inka proclaims. Chief Inkotoe gives the boys a somber look.

"Yes, your brave warriors have freed our village and saved

the medallion necklaces," Chief Inkotoe replies. Then he flashes a big smile and looks out to the villagers.

"This is a great victory for our people, we will celebrate with a festival!" Chief Inkotoe proudly announces. The villagers break out in cheers along with Calvin and Brad who are always ready to party. JJ and Inka share a smile as the group joyfully awaits the festival.

Chapter Seven

GOING HOME

It does not take long for the festival to begin. The villagers are performing a ceremonial dance similar to the traditional snake dance, except there are no snakes, and they are not praying for rain, it is just a festive dance. The villagers are lined up one after another and move like a snake through the center of the village as they dance to the rhythm of beating drums and chanting. At the end of line, or the snake's tail, Calvin and Brad are showing off their latest dance moves.

JJ and Inka are together watching the ongoing celebration with an occasional laugh after seeing a few crazy moves by Calvin and Brad. Inka looks at JJ and smiles.

"This is such a wonderful celebration; you and your friends are so brave. My father wants the warriors to know that they are welcome to stay at our village," Inka says. JJ is taken by the offer and gives Inka a smile.

"That's nice of your father, but we need to get home to our parents," JJ replies. He looks around and shrugs his shoulder, then looks at Inka. "We just don't know how to get home," JJ adds. Inka's puzzled and looks at JJ.

"You do not know where you came from?" a confused Inka responds. JJ points to South Mountain.

"We live on the other side of the mountain," JJ says. Inka looks at the mountain, then smiles at JJ.

"Then, that should be easy," an innocent Inka responds. JJ wishes it were that easy but feels he needs to try to explain to Inka. "Inka, a huge dust storm brought us to you, like it had magical powers," JJ says. "Calvin, Brad, and I are from a different time," he adds. Inka rears her head back and looks puzzled.

"A different time?" Inka asks curiously.

"Yeah, but I feel like I've known you forever, like…" Before JJ could finish, Inka gently reaches for JJ's hand.

"I know, JJ, I feel the same way, like we have a destiny," Inka says. JJ smiles at Inka, then picks a small branch off the ground and draws a figure of a heart in the dirt, then he writes "JJ x Inka" in the center. Inka gives JJ a smile.

"What does that mean?" a curious Inka asks.

"Oh, let's say it comes from the heart," JJ says with a smile. Inka returns the smile and gives JJ a hug. The two share their moment when suddenly a gentle breeze blows Inka's hair. JJ gazes out toward the horizon with a curious face.

"Hmm…looks like the wind is picking up…could it be?" JJ wonders aloud.

"Could what be?" a curious Inka asks. JJ gives Inka a serious look.

"Inka, this might sound crazy, but this might be the Magical Storm!" an anxious JJ responds. Inka gives JJ a puzzled look.

"JJ, I don't understand…a magical storm?" a confused Inka asks. JJ is torn with mixed feelings. He is experiencing strong emotions for Inka, but he knows if it is the Magical Storm, he will be leaving her for good.

"It's hard to understand, Inka, but I think this storm might be the only way we can get back home," JJ says. He looks out toward the storm while signaling to Calvin and Brad.

On the horizon a huge wall of dust is rolling over the desert. The wind has quickly picked up strength and is howling. Dust and debris start to sail through the village.

Toeteeko, wearing Brad's Cubs hat, runs up to JJ and Inka, followed closely by Calvin and Brad. The group is finally together, and JJ gives Calvin and Brad a serious look.

"Look, guys, we've got to get to the mountain and fast!" JJ announces as he points to the storm. "This might be the Magical Storm, and it may be our only chance to get home. We've got to give it a try!" JJ gives Toeteeko a serious look.

"Toeteeko, can you find us three horses?" an anxious JJ asks.

"I will do whatever you ask. I owe you much," replies Toeteeko. He dashes away.

The haboob storm is closer, and the wall of dust is towering. The howling wind is intense. The boys have overcome many obstacles and dangers, but now the Magical Storm has returned for a reason, unknown to the boys, to time travel them back to the present day.

Inka and the boys are staring out toward the storm and are anxiously waiting for Toeteeko's return. After several minutes Toeteeko runs up to the group holding three ropes, with only two horses. He has brought JJ's horse, the conquistador captain's horse, and unnoticed at first but behind the two horses at the end of a longer rope a droopy donkey.

"She's not a horse, but she's a very fast donkey," Toeteeko says with a smile as JJ takes hold of the three ropes.

"Good job, Toeteeko!" JJ says. He looks a Calvin and Brad. "Okay, fellas, get on." Brad gives JJ a puzzled look.

"Dude, I've never rode a horse before," Brad announces.

"No problem!" Calvin replies as he quickly gets on the captain's horse as Brad haplessly watches Calvin, then Brad looks at the donkey.

"A donkey!" Brad snaps. "I'm to ride a donkey?" JJ gives Brad an encouraging look.

"Come on, Brad, get on. We don't have much time!" JJ says. Brad gives JJ a wry look and jumps up on the donkey, then almost immediately he does a 180-degree slide to the donkey's under belly.

"JJ, I need some help!" Brad yells. Calvin, who is on the captain's horse, breaks out in laughter.

"Nice job, Lone Ranger," Calvin says with a snicker as JJ helps Brad reposition on the donkey. JJ helps Brad get on top of the donkey, then JJ gives Brad a stern look.

"Just hold on, Brad, whatever you do, just hold on!" JJ instructs. Brad gives JJ a head nod. So Calvin and Brad are on their animals and start to wave goodbye to Inka and Toeteeko.

"You two take care, and I hope your father enjoys the War Bird," Calvin says.

"Yeah, and thanks for everything, little buddy," Brad says to Toeteeko. JJ looks at Calvin and Brad with final instructions.

"Look, head toward the mountain. I'll catch up, now

get!" JJ says as he slaps the horse on its hind leg with his hand and then immediately slaps the donkey's hind leg. The horse takes off with a steady gallop, followed by the donkey with a fast trot. Brad struggles with the ride, and to make matters worse, he still has Calvin's backpack on, which is bouncing up and down smacking Brad in his back and then his head.

JJ turns to Inka and Toeteeko who are watching Calvin and Brad ride away.

"Toeteeko, you better get home," JJ says. Toeteeko gives JJ a smile. He starts to run, then stops and turns around.

"Thank you, JJ, for saving our people," Toeteeko replies, then dashes away toward the village. JJ and Inka are standing alone and close together as JJ holds the rope to the horse. It's a somber moment for them both.

"Inka, I have to go, but I'll never forget you…you'll always be in my dreams," JJ says. Inka gives JJ a soft smile.

"And you'll always be in mine," Inka responds. JJ and Inka hug, but while Inka was holding JJ by his waist, and unbeknown to JJ, she slips two objects in his left vest pocket.

"Thank you, my brave warrior," Inka says in JJ's ear, then with teary eyes, she gives JJ a kiss on the cheek. They exchange tender smiles, then JJ mounts his horse.

"Bye, Inka," a somber JJ says. They reach for each other's hands for the last time.

"I love you, Inka," JJ says. Inka smiles.

"And I love you, and always remember, JJ, we have a

destiny," Inka replies. JJ smiles as they let go of each other's hands. JJ is fighting his emotions but knows he must ride and takes off with a hard gallop. After a few seconds, he turns around to look for Inka one last time, but he only sees a massive wall of dust and no Inka.

JJ gallops up to the foot of the mountain near a hiking trail. He pulls the reins, stopping the horse, and jumps off. JJ worked his horse hard and pets the animal's neck in appreciation.

"Good work, boy, but you need to go," JJ says, then gives the horse a gentle hand slap on its hind leg. The horse responds and gallops away. Calvin pulls up to JJ and jumps off the horse.

"JJ, I'm a natural at this!" Calvin proclaims as he looks around. "Where's Brad?" JJ shrugs his shoulders.

"I thought he was with you," JJ replies as the two anxiously look out toward the coming storm. The sound of Brad yelling and moaning catches their ears, but there is no sight of Brad. Then suddenly Brad bursts through a cloud of dust erratically bouncing up and down. Behind Brad is the massive wall of dust.

JJ and Calvin are frantically waving and encouraging Brad's riding efforts.

"Hurry up, Brad, you're almost here!" JJ and Calvin shout together.

Brad finally trots up on the donkey and jumps off. Brad's face is covered with a cringe as he gingerly walks up to the boys. He's holding the back of his head with one hand and his lower back with the other.

"Dudes, the pain, I think I need a doctor!" Brad announces. Calvin chuckles as JJ anxiously looks out toward the massive wall of dust. The storm has become much stronger and is only about fifty yards away.

"Come on, let's head up this trail!" JJ firmly says. So the boys dash up the trail as the storm quickly approaches. JJ sees a small boulder up the trail, it's about the size of a kitchen table, but it's the only shelter available.

"Quick, follow me!" JJ calls out. He darts behind the boulder and is followed by Calvin and Brad. Within seconds the storm engulfs the boulder and vanishes it from sight. The wind and dust are blowing immensely, and the howling is deafening. When they think the storm couldn't get any worse, it starts to ease up, and the boulder comes into view, along with the boys. They are covered with dust but don't care.

"Who's going to look first?" an apprehensive Brad asks.

"Let's look together," Calvin suggests. The boys share a head nod.

"Okay, on the count of three…one, two, three!" JJ yells out. Simultaneously, the boys pop their heads out from behind the boulder and immediately get wide-eyed, cheering for joy.

"Yeah!" the boys are ecstatic and yell together.

A view of the city reveals the interstate, trucks, and cars.

In the sky, a passenger jet approaches the local airport for a landing.

They're all smiles and exchange high-fives. Then Brad pinches Calvin on the cheek. "Ouch, what was that for?!" Calvin asks. Brad shrugs his shoulders.

"I had to pinch somebody to make sure I wasn't dreaming!" Brad responds.

Calvin gives Brad a disgruntled look.

"Man, you're supposed to pinch yourself!" a perturbed Calvin says. JJ looks at Calvin and Brad.

"Come on guys, let's get to the top of the mountain and see if we're really home!" JJ enthusiastically says. The boys share a head nod and dart up the trail, hoping to see home.

On top of the mountain, the boys are panting hard, but they are delighted to see their neighborhood.

"Dudes, we made it!" a joyful Brad announces. Calvin pulls out his cell phone.

"Hey. I got service!" Calvin says. "I'm calling my parents." Calvin tabs the cell phone.

"Let's go!" JJ says as he heads down the trail followed by Calvin and Brad.

The boys run up to the parking lot and find Calvin's parents waiting. Calvin gives JJ and Brad a serious look.

"Hey, are we going to say anything about this?" Calvin asks. JJ shrugs his shoulders.

"Who's going to believe us?" JJ replies as Calvin nods his head.

"Really…this was just too incredible to explain," Calvin adds. JJ flashes a serious look at Calvin and Brad.

"For now, and forever, it's our adventure. Let's just go home, we can talk about it later," JJ suggests. The boys nod their heads in agreement.

"Sounds good to me, besides, I'm starving!" Brad says as he looks a Calvin. "How about a ride, Calvin?" Brad asks.

"Sure, how about you, JJ?" Calvin asks.

"Thanks, but I'm sure my mom's on her way," JJ replies. Calvin and Brad fist pump JJ and walk away toward Calvin's parents' vehicle. JJ tucks his thumbs into his vest pockets and lets out a big sigh of relief.

"Wow!" an exhilarated JJ says. Then unexpectedly he feels something in his left vest pocket. "What this?" JJ mutters to himself as he looks down to his vest pocket and pulls out two square stone rocks. He places the stones in his palm for a better look and gets wide-eyed. JJ takes a double look and sees carvings on the stones. Although JJ never really saw the gold medallion maps side-by-side, he realizes the stones are very similar to that of Inka's and her father's. JJ lowers his eyebrows and looks puzzled.

"Are these maps to the secret cave, and when did Inka give these to me, and why?" a curious JJ says.

Chapter Eight

SPIRITS VISIT

It's two weeks later as a crowd in southwestern attire sits in arena bleachers keeping their eyes busy. A banner on a fence reads Annual Arizona Junior Rodeo Tournament.

The crowd jumps to their feet as they respond with cheers and applause to the action on the rodeo grounds. Off to the side of the main group of attendees, an older rodeo fan stands up to applaud. He's using a newspaper on the bleacher bench as a seat cushion, and when a slight gust of wind blows, it turns the front page over revealing a second-page headline that reveals: "Gorge Mining Company to Bid on Sacred Indian Land." The male attendee sits back down with more cheers and applause.

On the rodeo grounds, JJ is fast galloping hard on Sadie as he weaves in and out around barrels. Horse hooves pound, and dirt kicks up as JJ and Sadie streak past the finish line followed by a trail of dust.

Calvin, Brad, Amy, and JJ's parents are jumping up and down cheering on JJ's performance. Dan checks his stopwatch and then cracks a small smile.

"Where did he learn to ride like that?" Dan mutters to himself. Calvin and Brad exchange fist bumps and look out toward JJ.

"Great time, JJ!" an enthusiastic Calvin yells out.

"Dude, way to go!" Brad adds. The parents give each other a hug and are obviously proud of JJ's run. Amy continues to jump up and down, cheering and applauding. There's a slightly high-pitched sound from the PA system, then the announcer speaks.

"Folks, we have a new champion," the announcer says. During the announcer's pause, JJ's parents share a hopeful smile. "It will be…JJ Garcia from Phoenix, Arizona!" Calvin and Brad give JJ's parents a high-five to celebrate their proud moment. Brad gives Amy a thumbs-up, but she returns the gesture with a sneer, rolling her eyes as she looks away shaking her head. You guessed it, Brad has a crush on Amy, an affection she isn't interested in, or just acts like it.

JJ slowly trots around the rodeo grounds and waves his hat, acknowledging the crowd. The crowd appreciates JJ's performance and responds with more cheers and applause. JJ leans forward near Sadie's ear as he pets the animal's neck.

"Good job, Sadie," JJ says. "That's my girl." No doubt

JJ has some heavy weight off his shoulders with the win and a trophy to bring back to the family ranch. But in JJ's heart and mind there's something that lingers, and that's the Magical Storm and his time with Inka.

Moments later Calvin and Brad are holding the back door to the horse trailer as JJ walks Sadie up a short ramp into the trailer.

"Come on, girl, just a little more," an encouraging JJ says as Sadie slowly enters the trailer for the trip home. As soon as she has totally entered the trailer, Calvin and Brad quickly close the door, then Calvin flips the lock securing the two back doors. JJ follows up by sliding the ramp under the trailer to complete the task. Calvin gives JJ a smile.

"Great run today, JJ!" Calvin says.

"Yeah, dude, you really worked it today!" Brad adds. JJ smiles and nods his head in appreciation to his friends. The boys are a team and always are giving each other encouragement, if not a hard time.

"Thanks, guys," JJ responds in a melancholy tone. Calvin and Brad share a somber glance.

"It's okay to be happy, JJ," Calvin says. JJ nods his head.

"Yeah, I know it's just...I'm confused," JJ says as he takes the two stone maps out of his pocket and blankly stares at them.

"Dude, you're thinking too much," Brad says. "You got to be like me."

"Yeah, be like Brad and just don't think," Calvin says

with a chuckle as the boys share a laugh.

Suddenly JJ senses a slight breeze in the air that gets his attention, and he curiously gazes out toward the southern horizon.

"Hmm…seems like the wind is picking up," a suspicious JJ mentions. Calvin and Brad notice JJ's attention is focused on the southern horizon as the wind gets noticeably stronger. The boys stare out as the trees starts to sway and the bushes rustle. They share curious looks when they see a faint dust line crossing the horizon.

"Boys, this trophy is a beauty," an elated Dan's voice is heard as JJ's parents and Amy walk up to the trailer. Dan is proudly holding the trophy, then extends the trophy to JJ.

"Here, you take it, JJ, and we'll get some lunch and celebrate!" Dan announces as Brad's eyes light up to the sound of food.

The group is gathered and all smiles when Dan looks out toward the southern horizon.

"Looks like a dust storm is headed this way," Dan proclaims. "Let's get into the truck and wait it out." The boys are looking very apprehensive as they get into the back seat of the truck because whatever is happening is happening quick.

On the southern horizon a huge, dark dust storm is rolling across the desert. The trees and bushes have quickly started to respond to the high winds as the trees bend. Dust and debris are blowing wildly, and the howling of the wind has ramped up as if a switch has been turned on.

JJ's dad looks surprised as he gazes out the window.

"Boy, this storm came up fast and out of nowhere!" Dan proclaims as the truck starts to shake and small rocks ping off the front windshield. In the back seat, the boys are uptight and nervously share a glance. Brad, who is in the middle, closes his eyes and crosses his fingers and looks as if he's praying. JJ and Calvin glance at Brad, then anxiously look at each other.

"Might as well," Calvin says. And it doesn't take long before Calvin and JJ have their eyes closed and fingers crossed as the truck trembles in the wind.

Outside, the truck and trailer are quickly becoming engulfed in the massive wall of dust. The wind blows violently and howls like a tornado. Within a second there is no sign of the truck and trailer, and the storm feels like it will last forever. Then suddenly the wind begins to ease up. A quick moment later, the truck and trailer come into view, and the wind stops.

Inside the truck, the boys share a glance, then flash big smiles and collectively let out a sigh of relief.

"Yeah, all right!" the boys shout out together. Brad looks like he just received his favorite Christmas present.

"Yes!" a joyful Brad says. "My prayers were answered, we're still here!"

Amy turns around and gives Brad a puzzled expression.

"What does that mean?" a quizzical Amy asks. At that point JJ knows he needs to intervene.

"Hey, it's Brad, it doesn't mean anything," JJ quickly responds. JJ and Calvin give Brad the evil eye. A second later, country rock fills the truck cab as the boys start to air jam in the back seat. Amy turns around and flashes a smirk expression, then she looks up at her mom.

"Boys are weird!" Amy proclaims. "Especially Brad." She flashes a devilish smile as the truck drives off.

The Garcia family is hanging out watching the local news on the television. Amy is asleep on the couch between her parents with her head on her mom's lap. JJ is lying on the rug next to Lucky as he uses his arm and hand to prop his head up. JJ lets out a big yawn.

"Well, it's bedtime for me," JJ announces as he gets up and hugs his mom and then his dad.

"Good night," a tired JJ says as he walks away from the couch.

"Great tournament today, son, we're proud of you," his dad says. JJ stops and turns around with a smile.

"Thanks Dad, it was special," JJ replies as he heads to his bedroom.

Stone map 1 and stone map 2.

It's later that night, and the room is dimly by a small night lamp on the dresser. The stone maps are a couple of inches apart from each other and in no particular order. The stone maps are special to JJ for the only reason they came from Inka.

JJ is sound asleep in his bed when suddenly something amazing happens. He hears Inka's voice.

"JJ, my warrior, do not be frightened, it's me, Princess Inka," Inka softly says. JJ's eyes quickly open and curiously scan the room.

"Inka?!" an inquisitive JJ responds. Inka is standing at the front of the bed next to JJ. He quickly sits up.

"Inka, what are you doing here?" a confused JJ asks as he takes a double look and shakes his head.

"I must be dreaming…no, I've got to be dreaming," JJ mutters to himself. He lies back in bed and closes his eyes. Then he suspiciously opens one eye and sees Inka is still standing by the side of his bed but closer. Inka gives JJ a smile.

"JJ, you're not dreaming. The storm today has brought my spirit to you," Inka explains. JJ sits up and rubs his eyes and flashes a puzzled look.

"This can't be… Inka, is this really you?" a dubious JJ asks. Inka smiles and sits down next to JJ.

"JJ, please listen, my people need your help. They'll be forced off their sacred land if nothing is done!" Inka announces. JJ is still half in a daze and very confused as he shakes his head. He somberly looks at Inka.

"But, Inka, what can I do?" JJ asks. Inka then gives JJ a serious look.

"The stone maps, JJ," Inka replies as JJ flashes a puzzled expression.

"The stone maps?!" JJ responds.

"Yes, JJ, after you told me about the storm, I knew it had magical powers. I realized then we have a destiny with each other," Inka explains. JJ rears his head back.

"A destiny?" a confused JJ asks. Inka gently nods her head and smiles.

"That is why I gave you a copy of the gold medallion maps. I knew someday there would come a time when you could use the stone maps to help my people JJ, and that time has come," Inka further explains.

"Inka, I keep the stone maps with me all the time… they remind me of you!" JJ proclaims.

"JJ, I need you to use the stone maps and find the secret cave, the gold will save my people," Inka says. JJ scratches his head.

"Save your people?" a confused JJ asks. Inka leans forward with a serious expression.

"The storm that brought you back to me has brought my spirit hundreds of years forward to you. It's our destiny, JJ, there's a reason for everything," Inka profoundly says. "And I know now my brave warriors have their own destiny with the Magical Storm." Inka gently touches JJ's cheek and kisses him on the forehead. Then she stands up and steps back.

"I must go now, but remember, I will always love you," Inka finishes as she continues to step back, then fades away. JJ shakes his head and rubs his eyes.

"Boy, I better get some sleep," JJ mutters to himself. He lies back down and closes his eyes, then he opens one eye and scans the room.

"Nay," JJ says as he closes his eyes and falls back to sleep.

It's late at night in Brad's bedroom. He's asleep and shares his pillow with his favorite Chicago Cubs teddy bear. All is quiet except for the rumbling noise of Brad snoring. Above his single-shelf headboard are six karate belts of different colors: white, yellow, orange, green, blue, and a brown one. Each belt represents a different rank or achievement. They're lined up side-by-side hanging individually from a hook. A seventh hook is empty, which is where Brad plans to hang his black belt someday. Below the seventh hook on the headboard shelf is a picture of a US Army soldier, Brad's dad.

Toeteeko's spirit is standing at the foot of the bed. He is wearing the Chicago Cubs hat that Brad give him and looks at Brad with a smile. Brad rolls over to his other side and continues to snore. At the foot of the bed, Toeteeko is gone, but he left the Cubs hat hanging from the bedpost.

A four-motor solar-powered drone sits on a small table under the softly lit lamp. It's nighttime in Calvin's room, and Chief Inkotoe is standing next to the table admiring the drone. He nods his head, then places a palm leaf like the type used on the War Bird on the table. He walks over to the head of the bed where Calvin is fast asleep. Next to

Calvin is a bedside table with his glasses and an Eagle Scout survival handbook within close reach. Chief Inkotoe looks down at Calvin and smiles. He nods his head, and just like that, he is gone.

The morning sunlight is shining in JJ's face as he sleeps. He opens his eyes and quickly sits up in bed.

"Wow, what a dream!" an excited JJ says. He jumps out of bed and walks over to the dresser to look at the stone maps. Suddenly, he gets wide-eyed and steps back.

"Huh, I didn't leave the stone maps like this," a puzzled JJ responds. He takes a step closer to the dresser and curiously takes another look.

"No way, it was a dream…wasn't it?" JJ mutters to himself as he continues to inspect the stone maps. But unbeknown to JJ, the stone maps are side-by-side and positioned to reveal the directions to the secret cave. Before JJ realizes what has happened, he grabs the stone maps off the dresser and intensely stares at them in his hand. JJ is confused and just shakes his head.

"The guys aren't going to believe me," a somber JJ says. "They'll think I'm crazy or something."

Brad is getting out of bed. He stretches his arms and lets out a big yawn.

"Aah," Brad grunts out as he looks around his room. "What's that?" he says as his eyes focus on the Cubs hat hanging from the bedpost. He walks over to the hat, and after a brief pause of staring at the hat, he grabs it from the bedpost for a better look.

"Looks just like it," Brad comments. He tosses the hat onto his bed and walks toward the bedroom door. Brad stops and turns around and takes a quick glance at the hat.

"Mr. Funny Man, Calvin, anything for a joke," Brad says as he walks away.

It's morning, and Calvin is sitting on the side of his bed. He reaches for his glasses and puts them on. Then he walks over to admires his latest project, a drone, and sees the palm leaf. Calvin cracks a smile.

"Oh, a palm leaf, hmm…how did that get here?" Calvin says in gest. "Of course, Mr. Comedian, Brad!" He nonchalantly tosses the palm leaf back onto the table, then pushes his glasses up off his nose. Calvin sports a big smile and picks the drone up for its morning inspection.

"Yes, what a beauty!" Calvin starts off. "Solar powered, remote controlled, totally disassembles in seconds…with retractable claw, camera, and built-in monitor screen in the remote-control panel!" a proud Calvin says as he readjusts his glasses while keeping a big smile. Suddenly his cell phone that he keeps on his worktable at night starts to beep. He places the drone back on the table and grabs his phone to read the message.

"Meet at the park, ASAP, JJ," Calvin mutters to himself as he flashes a puzzled expression.

"Hmm…what's the rush?" Calvin wonders out loud. Then within a quick moment, the cell phone starts to beep again. He takes a closer look at the phone.

"It's Brad," Calvin says. "Ha, ha, ha, Mr. Funny Man, see you at the park." Calvin flashes a dumbfounded expression.

"What's that mean?" Calvin ponders. "Mr. Funny Man?" Calvin curiously stares off.

It's midmorning, and JJ and Calvin are sitting on the seats of a swing set. Calvin looks around, then looks at JJ.

"Hey, so where's Brad?" Calvin asks. JJ shrugs his shoulders.

"Well, he's late as usual," JJ replies as the two boys patiently wait for Brad.

"Excuse me!" Brad voice barks from behind JJ and Calvin. "Has anyone seen my Cubs hat!" JJ and Calvin are startled and caught off guard; they quickly turn around to look at Brad.

"Your old Cubs hat?" Calvin asks. "That my friend would be impossible." Brad is getting irritable and thinks JJ and Calvin, especially Calvin, is messing with him. His eyes tense up and his lips tighten.

"Yeah, like you guys don't know what I mean, Calvin!" Brad defensively yells out. JJ and Calvin exchange puzzled looks and jump off the seats. Calvin gives Brad a stern look.

"Okay, Mr. Comedian, nice job sneaking the palm leaf into my room!" a defiant Calvin snaps back. Calvin and Brad are slowly inching closer and closer to a point they're almost in each other's face. JJ is getting suspicious.

"What are you saying, Brad?" JJ says as Brad gives him a serious look.

"Dude, my Cubs hat!" Brad strongly responds. "Calvin must have found an identical copy and hung it on my bedpost, and I saw it there this morning. Come on!" Brad is getting more aggressive, and Calvin is reaching his tipping point.

"I didn't hang no Cubs hat on your bedpost!" Calvin snaps back. JJ sees it's time to intervene before the situation goes south.

"Okay, okay, I got a question to ask you guys," JJ says as he gets ready for the big inquiry.

"Did anyone have a strange dream last night?" JJ asks. Calvin and Brad share a puzzled look, then Calvin addresses JJ.

"Strange dream, what do you mean?" Calvin asks as

Brad stares off pondering the question.

"Hmm…strange dream, last night?" Brad wonders out loud. JJ gives Calvin and Brad a serious face.

"Look, I'm going to tell you guys something and don't think I'm crazy. Just hear me out," JJ says as Calvin and Brad attentively look at JJ.

"The storm yesterday brought Inka's spirit to me last night," JJ announces. Calvin and Brad share a puzzled glance and then give JJ a quizzical look.

"What?!" the two say together. JJ pauses and nods his head.

"Yeah, at first, I thought it was a dream, but in the morning, I realized she rearranged the two stone maps to reveal the directions to the secret cave!" JJ explains.

"So…what did she say?" a curious Calvin asks.

"She's asking for help. We need to use the stone maps and find the gold," JJ continues to explain. He gives Calvin and Brad a serious look.

"Her people are in trouble, and we're the only ones with maps to the secret cave," JJ adds. Calvin gets wide-eyed at the thought of the secret cave and gives JJ a deep inquisitive look.

"You mean you know where the secret cave is?" a curious Calvin asks.

"Yeah…but no. I picked them up before I realized what really happened," JJ says as he shakes his head. Brad gives JJ a wry smile.

"Dude!" Brad responds as JJ innocently shrugs his shoulders. "Do you have a little idea how she laid out the stones?" Brad adds. JJ sports a pathetic smile and shakes his head no.

"I know…but that's why I texted you guys, I wanted to know if anything strange happened last night," JJ says. Calvin and Brad share a slack-jawed glance as they both realize what's going on.

"Are you telling me…Chief Inkotoe was in my room last night?" an apprehensive Calvin asks as Brad starts to get fidgety.

"Wait, wait…Toeteeko really brought my hat back?" an anxious Brad asks. Calvin gives Brad a somber look.

"Brad, trust me, we had nothing to do with your hat," Calvin states. Brad looks beside himself.

"I can't believe it; a ghost was in my room!" Brad says as his eyes roll back in his head, and he faints, falling to the ground. JJ and Calvin share a glance and a smile.

"Well, that's our Brad," Calvin says with a chuckle.

"Yeah, but look, Calvin, we need to do some serious research on Inka's people," a determined JJ proclaims. Calvin nods his head.

"Okay, my house at six tonight," Calvin says.

"Prefect!" JJ responds.

It's the same day, about noon, in the downtown business

district, and a sign on an office door reads Bureau of Native American Land Management. Inside the office a neat stack of one-hundred-dollar bills fill a briefcase. Suddenly a hand pushes the briefcase across the top of a business desk.

Sitting across the desk is T. W. Hooker, a man in his midfifties and the Director of Native American Land Management. Hooker is a short, heavyset, bald man who is wearing a standard black business suit. He has a questionable history and is a very greedy person. Across the desk is Mr. Jones, the owner of Gorge Mining Company. He sports slick, combed-back gray hair and wears a high-end Gucci-style black business suit. He is a man without scruples and runs his company the same way. Standing directly behind him in dark sunglasses are his two bodyguards.

"Well, Mr. Hooker, as you can see, Gorge Mining Company certainly likes doing business with you…again," Mr. Jones says as Mr. Hooker shuffles in his chair.

"Yes indeed, Mr. Jones, but remember, for legal purposes, the bidding will remain open until this next Monday," Mr. Hooker responds.

"I understand, Mr. Hooker," Mr. Jones replies. Mr. Hooker relaxes in his chair and gives Mr. Jones a confident smile.

"Good, and once you win the bid, the current residents have only thirty days to vacate the land," Mr. Hooker explains as Mr. Jones flashes a cocky smile.

"Like I said, Mr. Hooker, it's been a pleasure doing

business with you," Mr. Jones concludes with a soft, sinister chuckle. The two men stand up, share a smile, and shake hands.

Later that evening, sometime past six o'clock, Calvin and JJ are sitting on the side of Calvin's bed and are busy with Calvin's laptop. Brad is standing next to Calvin's project desk and is checking out Calvin's drone. He smiles and nods his head.

"Dude, this is really cool!" Brad says. Calvin gives Brad a quick glance and smiles as he accepts the compliment.

"Thanks, it's my latest," Calvin responds. Brad lets out a chuckle.

"I'm sure its solar powered," Brad says with a hint of sarcasm.

"Of course, renewable energy," Calvin responds as Brad picks up the drone for a better look.

"Yeah, very cool… Hey, can you launch anything from it?" a curious Brad asks. Calvin's eyes narrow, and he pushes his glasses up off his nose as he gives the question some serious thought.

"That's not a bad idea," Calvin mutters to himself. Suddenly JJ gets wide-eyed.

"Hey, Calvin, read this!" an excited JJ says. Calvin quickly sits back down on the bed with JJ and looks at the laptop screen. Then he begins to read out loud.

"'Local authorities say the bidding for the federal land currently occupied by the Hopi tribe of Arizona will be finalized in the coming week,'" Calvin reads, then gives JJ a serious look and continues to read. "Authorities state, Gorge Mining Company remains the top bidder.'" JJ and Calvin exchange a serious glance. JJ quickly jumps up and realizes what's going on.

"That it! That's what Inka was trying to tell me... We need to find the gold and outbid this Gorge Mining Company!" JJ proclaims. Calvin nods his head.

"I guess we're visiting the federal building tomorrow," Calvin adds. Brad continues to examine the drone. Then he sets it down and gives JJ and Calvin a dubious look.

"Yeah, right, like who's going to talk to us?" Brad asks. JJ's eyes narrow, and his lips tighten as he stares off, then within a moment, he cracks a half smile and nods his head.

"Hmm...I've got a plan, let's meet at the bus stop at nine first thing!" JJ announces. Calvin and Brad nod their heads in agreement.

The three boys are standing in the lobby of the Arizona Federal Building, examining the directory. They're looking for the name of the person in charge of Native American Land Management when suddenly JJ gets wide-eyed.

"Here, it's a guy named T. W. Hooker, and his office is on the fourth floor—let's go!" JJ eagerly says. So the boys dash toward the elevator and are on their way to the fourth floor determined to help Inka and her people.

The boys are standing outside of an office door staring at the title on the door that reads T. W. Hooker - Director of Native American Land Management. JJ confidently nods his head.

"Okay, let me do the talking," JJ announces as he opens the door and enters. Calvin and Brad share wry smiles and begin to follow JJ. But Brad can't resist an opportunity to bug Calvin. So as Calvin enters the doorway, Brad quickly enters at the same time, jamming their shoulders in the doorway frame. Brad chuckles and gives Calvin a big smile. Calvin flashes an annoyed expression and just shakes his head.

"I hate when you do that," Calvin grumbles.

The boys are standing next to a short wall that separates them from the receptionist. The receptionist is sitting at her desk and busy on a computer. She has her back to the boys and has not acknowledged their presence.

"Excuse me, ma'am," JJ says. The receptionist stops her work and quickly half spins her chair around to look at the boys. She gives them a once-over and flashes a snobbish expression.

"Can I help you?" the irritable receptionist says. JJ gives a polite smile to the receptionist.

"Yes, ma'am, we're the representatives from the JJ Garcia

Group, and we have an eleven o'clock appointment with Mr. Hooker," JJ calmly says. The receptionist rears her head back.

"They sent three boys?!" the puzzled receptionist mutters out loud. JJ smiles and nods his head.

"Yes, ma'am," JJ replies. The receptionist shakes her head and fusses with some papers on her desk.

"Well, wait here and I'll inform Mr. Hooker that you have arrived for your appointment," the grumpy receptionist responds. She gets up and quickly walks to Mr. Hooker's office door, then she opens the door and gives the boys a perturbed look before she enters Mr. Hooker's office. Calvin and Brad are giving JJ a mischievous look.

"The JJ Garcia Group?! Well…excuse me!" Brad says. JJ gives Brad an innocent look and shrugs his shoulders.

"Come on, you didn't think we were going to walk right in here without an appointment!" JJ replies as Calvin gives JJ a nod of confidence.

"Great thinking, I like it, the JJ Garcia Group," Calvin responds. "I've always wanted to be a CEO."

The office door quickly opens as the receptionist steps into the doorway.

"Mr. Hooker will see you boys now," the receptionist announces. JJ and Calvin share a smile, then walk past the receptionist followed by Brad. Brad stops and gives the receptionist a smile.

"Any donuts?" Brad jokingly asks. The receptionist gives Brad a perturbed look and slams the door.

Mr. Hooker is standing next to his desk as the boys enter the office for their appointment. Mr. Hooker politely smiles at the boys.

"Welcome, gentlemen, have a seat," Mr. Hooker says. The boys walk over to three empty chair that are lined up side-by-side in the front of the desk. JJ leads the way as the boys find their seats.

"Well, boys, excuse me…gentlemen, what can I do for you today?" Mr. Hooker says. JJ leans forward slightly.

"Mr. Hooker, we understand you're the person we need to talk to if we want to bid on a land proposal," JJ asks. Mr. Hooker gives JJ a smile.

"Yes, young man, I would be that person," Mr. Hooker replies.

"Well, then we would like to bid on some federal land in northern Arizona," JJ announces. The smile leaves Mr. Hooker's face as his eyes narrow and a quizzical expression covers his face.

"Hmm…and which northern Arizona land bid are you referring to?" a curious Mr. Hooker asks. JJ shares a glance with Calvin and Brad, then gives Mr. Hooker a serious look.

"The land bid which is currently occupied by the Hopi tribe," JJ calmly answers. Mr. Hooker ruffles in his chair as his one eyebrow rises in a curious fashion. He gives JJ a serious look.

"May I ask you, how did you become aware of this bid?" Mr. Hooker inquires.

"We researched it, sir!" JJ quickly responds. Mr. Hooker slowly rears his head back.

"I see…and you think you have the money for a competitive bid?" Mr. Hooker asks. JJ puts his hands together with his fingers interlocking as he rests his forearms on the table.

"I believe we do, and I feel comfortable we'll be the highest bidder," JJ states in a confident manner. Mr. Hooker flashes a serious face and aggressively leans forward, giving JJ a stern look.

"Look, young man, we're talking several million dollars!" Mr. Hooker states. JJ continues to remain calm and gives Mr. Hooker a smile.

"We understand," JJ replies. Mr. Hooker quickly gets up from his chair and abruptly walks over to the office window and stares down to the street traffic. Well, that's all Calvin and Brad needed to see as they share mischievous smiles. Within a second Calvin starts to wiggle his hands from his ears while sticking his tongue out. Brad is trying his best from laughing out loud and decides to join the antics. He crosses his arms and pushes his chest out while sporting a sour face. JJ gives the two a perturbed look and shakes his head, all along trying not to laugh.

Meanwhile, Mr. Hooker continues to stare out the window and appears deep in thought.

"Okay, but you boys better not be wasting my time!" Mr. Hooker harshly responds. "By law, I have to accept your intent to submit a bid." Mr. Hooker walks back to his desk and sits down. Then he opens a desk drawer and pulls out a paper form. He gives JJ a disturbed look and hands the paper form to JJ as Calvin and Brad watch with innocent smiles.

"Fill this Intent to Bid form out with the name of your organization…and I'll need the addresses of where you can be located," Mr. Hooker says with a devious tone. JJ inspects the form, then lowers the form and gives Mr. Hooker a smile.

"May I borrow your pen?" JJ asks. Mr. Hooker flashes a smirk from the side of his mouth and reaches into his suit pocket. He grabs a pen and starts to hand it to JJ, then suddenly stops.

"Just one last thing, the bidding ends noon this Monday, and the top bid is currently seven million dollars…any questions?" Mr. Hooker asks as he resumes to hand the pen over to JJ. JJ grabs the pen and quickly fills out the Intent to Bid form and hands the pen back to Mr. Hooker.

"No questions, sir. I think we know what we need to do, and we appreciate your time, thank you," JJ replies. Mr. Hooker's eyebrows lower and his lips tighten as he looks toward the door and head gestures for the boys to leave. The boys get it and get out of their chairs and walk to the door. Calvin opens the door and walks out of the office followed by Brad. JJ begins to walk through the doorway, then stops and looks at Mr. Hooker with an apprehensive expression. They share a glance, then JJ leaves, shutting the door. Mr. Hooker immediately grabs the phone and starts to dial, then places the phone by his ear.

"Jones, it's Hooker, look, we have a big problem, and you need to get rid of it… Before I explain, write down these addresses!" Mr. Hooker anxiously says.

The boys are waiting at the bus stop after their appointment. Calvin and Brad feel the meeting went well, but Calvin notices JJ appears somewhat apprehensive.

"So, what do you think?" Calvin asks. JJ's eyes narrow, and he rubs his chin. He gives Calvin and Brad a serious look.

"There's something fishy about that guy," JJ proclaims. "But never mind, we've got to get to the Superstition Mountains." JJ stares off pondering the next move. Suddenly Calvin gets wide-eyed.

"I got it!" Calvin announces. "I need a two-night campout for one of my merit badges, and I'll tell my parents this is a good weekend for it, and you guys are going with me." JJ gives Calvin a smile and nods his head.

"Sounds good to me," JJ says.

"I'm in," Brad adds. The boys high five each other as the bus pulls up.

Chapter Nine

SEARCH FOR THE GOLD

It's midmorning Saturday, and Tom Jackson's Ford Explorer is in a desert parking lot. The boys are loaded with camping gear and are standing next to the driver's side window. Unknown to Brad, his backpack is larger with the word TENT stenciled across the top. In the background is desert terrain and the towering Superstition Mountains with an elevation of 5,024 feet above sea level. With the Valley of the Sun at approximately 1,076 feet above sea level, the Superstition Mountains rest at about 3,000 feet elevation over the Phoenix Metropolitan area. The mountain anchors the western portion of the Superstition Mountains, a range that covers 160,000 acres and was formed from intense volcanic activity some twenty-nine million years ago. The western face of the mountain has a steep, vertical drop of about 1,800 feet.

Calvin smiles at his dad as the boys get ready for their search.

"Okay, Dad, thanks for the ride. I'll use Brad's cell phone and keep in touch," Calvin says.

"You boys be safe and good scouting!" Calvin's dad replies. The driver's window goes up, and the vehicle pulls away. The boys start to walk away side-by-side toward the beginning of a trail known as Peralta Trail. They're taking the surroundings in, and after about ten minutes, JJ stops and gives Calvin and Brad a glance.

"Let's find a rest area and take a break, I'd like to look at the maps before we go much farther," JJ says. Calvin and Brad nod their heads in agreement.

"Sounds good, I can conduct some aerial flight patterns," Calvin replies. Brad perks up.

"Cool, you brought the drone?" an excited Brad asks. Calvin flashes a thumbs-up.

"Yeah, and I've incorporated a special new feature," Calvin announces.

"Super cool!" Brad responds. "Hey, by the way, why is my backpack so much bigger than your guys'?" JJ and Calvin share a smile, then Calvin looks at Brad.

"Oh, I forgot, you got the tent," Calvin answers. Brad rears his head back and looks curious.

"What happened to sleeping under the stars?" Brad mutters out loud as the boys share a laugh.

"Hey look, there's a park bench!" JJ announces as the boys continue their hike.

Meanwhile, the Ford Explorer is pulling out of the parking lot and onto a road and headed to the main highway about seven miles away. As the vehicle pulls out, it passes a black Cadillac SUV that is parked alongside the parking lot entrance. The SUV slowly take off and heads down the road to the parking lot. The vehicle enters the parking lot and drives up to the start of the trail. A sign at the beginning of the trail reads Peralta Trailhead. The vehicle stops.

Inside the SUV are five men. Mack the leader who is holding a cell phone and sits in the driver's seat. Next to him in the passenger seat is Sam, his associate who has been watching the boys with his binoculars. In the back seat are three bodyguards dressed in black wearing dark sunglasses. The group are Mr. Jones's Gorge Mining hit men and have been ordered to follow the boys. Mack brings the cell phone to his mouth.

"Mr. Jones, we followed the boys to the Superstition Mountains. It looks like one of the parents dropped them off," Mack reports.

"The Superstition Mountains! What are they up to?" Mr. Jones responds over the cell phone. Mack shrugs his shoulders.

"Well, they're headed up a trail, and they sure have plenty of camping gear," Mack informs.

"Mack, listen, it's hit time and make it look like a hunting accident. You got it?" Mr. Jones commands as Mack nods his head.

"Yeah, boss, I got it," Mack replies as Mr. Jones's cell phone goes quiet. Mack stares out the window, then gives Sam a serious look.

"Sam, get the drone ready. You and the men are going for a hike," Mack announces.

Calvin, with a remote control in his hands, and Brad are standing together at one end of a picnic table checking out Calvin's drone. JJ is sitting at the other end of the picnic table with an empty face as he stares down at the two stone maps that are resting on a paper map of the trails and mountains that make up the Superstition Mountains Park. Suddenly the drone lifts off and features Calvin's new incorporation, two long cylindrical tubes, one on each side. Within no time Calvin has the drone conducting impressive aerial maneuvers that include loops and figure eights. Then the drone steadily hovers directly above the picnic table at about fifteen feet and gradually descends with a smooth landing. Calvin and Brad share a smile.

"Dude, that was awesome!" Brad proclaims as Calvin confidently nods his head while giving his drone the final inspection.

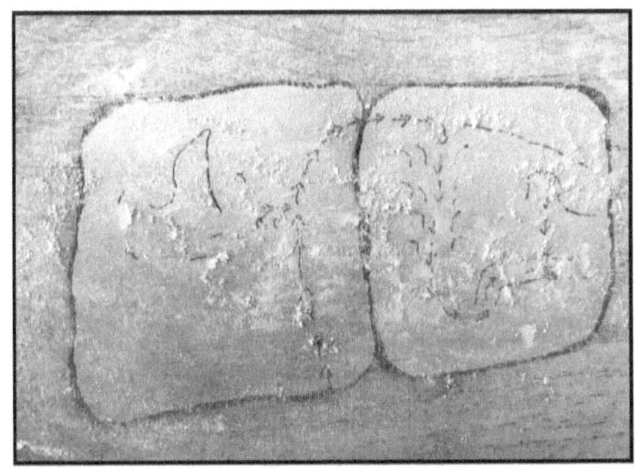

"Looks good to go," Calvin replies. Still, at the other end of the table, JJ continues to agonize over the two stone maps. He knows in the back of his mind he has seen the two stone maps correctly placed side-by-side, but as hard as he tries to remember, he draws a blank.

He sits in deep thought and just shakes his head.

"Hmm…how did Inka have these stone maps arranged?" JJ mutters to himself as he presses the issue. His face grows tense as his eyes close, trying to recall the night of Inka's spiritual visit. In JJ's mind a haze surrounds the stones, and the vision just isn't clear. Then he recalls that what appeared as arrows from the first stone aligned with arrows from the second stone. JJ quickly opens his eyes and anxiously starts manipulating the stone maps.

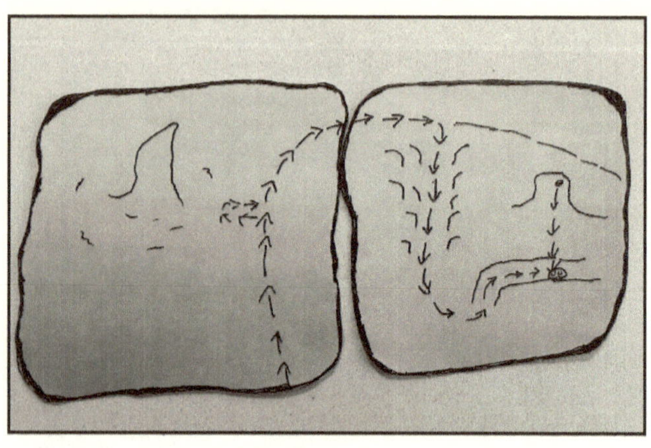

"Could this be it?" JJ wonders out loud. "There's only one arrangement where arrows from the first stone align with arrows from the second stone." JJ places the stones side-by-side and thinks he has found the pattern. Suddenly he gets wide-eyed.

"That's it!" an excited JJ announces. "That's how Inka had the stone maps arranged on my dresser." He jumps to his feet as Calvin and Brad rush over to JJ's side of the table.

"What's up?" a curious Calvin asks as JJ points to the stone maps.

"Look!" JJ says. Calvin and Brad stare down as JJ points out his discovery and a new set of hiking trails. All along Brad is busy chewing on a candy bar and stuffs the candy bar wrapper into his back pants pocket.

"We're going to Bluff Trail, the arrows seem to point toward Weaver's Needle Mountain, then they point northeast before pointing south!" an enthusiastic JJ announces. Calvin nods his head as he studies the new route on the paper map.

"Sounds like a plan and the hike is just a couple of miles. I'll double-check directions with my compass along the way," Calvin adds. "But why do the arrows seem to go about only halfway on the trail to Weaver's Needle Mountain?" a curious Calvin asks. JJ gives Calvin a serious look.

"Well, who knows, but I think we should follow the arrows. And we just need to use the trails that fit their pattern," JJ says. The two boys exchange smiles and are feeling somewhat confident they're on the right path. So they start to hike up the Bluff Spring Trail that will take them toward the Weaver's Needle Mountain area, but unbeknown to Brad, his candy bar wrapper falls out of his back pocket.

It's later in the morning as Sam and his three hit men are gathered by the same park bench the boys used earlier. Sam's main associate is Squeeze, a short, pudgy character. Working under Squeeze is Rocco, a normal-built guy who is carrying a square metallic suitcase that contains a drone. The other bodyguard under Squeeze is Boomer. He's the muscles of the group and does most of the dirty work. All three men are dangerous and carry a side arm. Squeeze bends over and picks up Brad's candy bar wrapper and holds it in front of Sam.

"Sam, looks like those troublemakers were here," Squeeze announces. Sam, who still has the binoculars hanging from his neck, also has a walkie-talkie clipped to his belt. He grabs the candy bar wrapper from Squeeze and gives it a serious look.

"We're closing in, let's get them," Sam says as he stares off, nodding his head with a sinister smile.

It's been about an hour, and the boys have made it to an intersect of two trails. Above them the drone is set in "Follow Me Status" and will hover above Calvin until he needs to use the remote control.

The boys have stopped to look at the stone maps and gaze out toward the landmark known as Weaver's Needle Mountain. It's about 1,000 feet tall and was formed when volcanic magma hardened inside a volcano forming a plug. After millions of years, erosion has removed the surrounding rock and sediment while the erosion-resistant plug remains, resulting in this distinctive landmark. JJ glances at the first stone and then back out toward the landmark.

"The carving on the first stone map reveals Weaver's Needle Mountain," a curious JJ says. Calvin pushes his glasses up off his nose.

"But the arrows point to the landmark, then seem to point back here!" a puzzled Calvin says as JJ diligently examines the first stone map.

"Yeah, that's strange, and the name of trail is Terrapin," a curious JJ explains. Brad is fussing with the tent backpack straps and gives them a strong tug. "Hey, it's a diversion. I bet they wanted people to think the gold is around here," Brad proclaims. JJ and Calvin exchange quizzical looks.

"He might be right!" a surprised JJ says. "A lot of people think the Lost Dutchman's Mine is near Weaver's Needle Mountain." JJ eyes narrow as he studies the stone maps.

"Dudes, who is going to hull heavy bags of gold out that far. Besides, this place looks dangerous. There's crazy terrain, jagged rocks, and canyons all over…forget it!" Brad adds. Calvin gives JJ a grin.

"Sometimes he baffles me," Calvin says as JJ shrugs his shoulders.

"He's making sense. They could have planted some gold here and there to keep people from the main cave, but let's stick with the plan and follow the arrows," JJ concludes. Calvin is checking his compass with the paper map and looks toward the east.

"Well, it looks like we stay on Bluff Spring Trail headed east until it becomes the Dutchman's Trail that heads sort of southeast," Calvin announces. JJ and Brad nod their heads in agreement as the boys resume their hike on Bluff Spring Trail.

After about an hour, the trail starts to bend southward. JJ suddenly stops and gives the second stone a curious look.

"This is interesting, I think we're on the Dutchman's Trail, but the arrows don't stay on the trail," JJ ponders out loud. Calvin reaches for the second stone map.

"Here, let me check it out," Calvin says. He places the stone maps on the paper map and aligns his compass. Then his eyes tighten as he rubs his chin.

"Wow, the arrows head straight south from here, like totally off the trail," a curious Calvin explains. JJ nods his head.

"I think the arrows are taking us through a canyon. It would make sense that sooner or later they would look for a cave in some unsuspected area," JJ proclaims as he reaches for the second stone from Calvin who hands them over to JJ. JJ studies the second stone with tense eyes. He gives Calvin a serious look.

"Calvin, do you see anything on the paper map that looks like this L-shaped pattern on the stone?" a curious JJ asks. Calvin intently examines the paper map. Then he slides the magnifying glass from the back of the compass and brings the map closer for review. Calvin looks at JJ and shakes his head.

"That's interesting. It looks like this canyon comes up to

a basin area, but there's no indication of any geographically L-shaped pattern on the map," a puzzled Calvin replies.

JJ and Calvin share a curious look. JJ looks south down the canyon.

"Well, let's keep hiking and get to the basin area," JJ says. "It shouldn't be that much farther." Brad is slightly lagging and trying his best to keep pace.

"Dudes!" Brad calls out as the sound of "dudes" echoes in the canyon. The echo has caught Brad's attention, and he cracks a smile and looks around.

Somewhere on the trail, Sam and the three hit men have gathered as Sam desperately scans the area. He lowers the binoculars and gives Squeeze a disturbed look.

"I lost them. Squeeze, I thought you had an eye on those kids!" an irritable Sam asks. Squeeze shrug his shoulders and gives Sam a helpless expression.

"I don't know, boss, they were just ahead of us less than a mile, then all of a sudden, they're gone!" Squeeze replies. Sam shakes his head and brings the binoculars to his eyes.

"This is just great," Sam mutters to himself.

Back down in the canyon, JJ and Calvin study the second stone and paper maps. Brad is amused with the echo and has decided to have some fun.

"That was awesome," Brad mutters to himself as he sports a devious look.

"Here's Brad!" He barks out his name and listens to it echo throughout the canyon. Calvin turns around and gives Brad a perturbed look.

"Hey, can you cut it out?" Calvin requests. Brad just looks at him and smiles.

At the trail, the word *Brad* echoes out from the canyon that is near Sam and his men. Sam lowers his binoculars, revealing a face with a suspicious expression as he and his men all look toward the canyon entrance.

"Boss, did you hear that?" an anxious Squeeze says as Sam stares at the canyon entrance, which is nothing more than an obscured small trail.

"Yeah, I heard it…let's go!" Sam eagerly replies as he walks to the canyon entrance followed by Squeeze and the two hit men.

Meanwhile the three boys are hiking through the canyon that appears to end and open to a basin area.

"Looks like this is the end of the canyon just like the map would indicate. We should be walking up to a basin area soon," Calvin announces. It didn't take long for the boys to step out of the tight canyon as the open area brings the sunshine and vegetation.

"Up the basin and we can take a break," JJ adds. Brad grabs the tent backpack straps and smiles.

"Sounds good to me, I've had it with this tent," Brad informs them as the three boys hike up the basin area past a line of trees and bushes to the left of them. After about fifteen minutes, the boys reach the top of the basin and are totally caught by surprise by what they missed. JJ and Calvin share a bewildered glance as they stare down to what appears to be the opening of the ravine.

"Man, we walked right by it!" a baffled Calvin replies as JJ examines the second stone maps. JJ gives Calvin a serious look.

"The trees and bushes hide this from us," a puzzled JJ says. "This may be the ravine that's carved on the second stone maps." So the boys share curious glances and start to walk down the ravine with an incline of about thirty degrees. The ravine is L-shaped with the first portion. The section the boys are hiking down is about twenty yards wide and about forty yards to the bottom. The walls are solid rock and gradually get taller as the boys descend. The wall to their left starts out just a couple of feet and ends with a wall that's fifteen feet high with a group of boulders. Along the wall a ledge about five feet high runs the course of the wall and is partially hidden by various bushes and other vegetation. After a brief hike, the boys reach the bottom of the ravine.

"This must be the other section of the L-shape on the

stone," says JJ as he looks down the length of the ravine.

"Looks about sixty yards in length and gradually ramps back up to the desert," JJ adds. Calvin scans the area as he nods his head.

"The long wall coming out of those boulders looks about fifteen feet high, but the walls nearest the basin vary," Calvin says as the boys walk down the ravine. Brad stops and takes his tent backpack off and wanders away from JJ and Calvin who are examining the second stone. JJ looks around of his surroundings. Calvin gives JJ a serious look.

"You know what's strange?" Calvin asks. JJ continues to check out the surroundings, then gives Calvin a serious look. Off to the side, Brad gets into his baseball pitcher's stance.

"What's that?" JJ responds as the sound of a dull thud fills the ravine as Brad just pitched a rock against the wall.

"Dudes, I'll tell you what's strange…we just hiked three sides of a circle!" Brad proclaims in the background. Calvin looks over to Brad and shakes his head.

"A sphere has no edges!" Calvin responds. "So, no sides." Brad gives Calvin a wry look.

"I said circle, not sphere!" Brad shoots back. Calvin rolls his eyes and shakes his head.

"Geez," Calvin mutters. JJ cracks a smile, then continues to examine the second stone.

He scopes out the ravine and gives Calvin a serious look.

"You know…Brad does come up with some interesting points," JJ says. Calvin rears his head back.

"Anyhow, Inka's dad follows a group of soldiers out into the Superstition Mountains, then he follows them down this canyon where he hides and finishes the carving on the second stone," JJ explains. Calvin gives JJ a quizzical look.

"I'm kind of following you, then what?" a curious Calvin asks as JJ looks toward the corner where the two large ravine walls meet that start the L-shape.

"Well, he needed a location where he could see all the activity," JJ says as he points toward the corner. Calvin looks toward the corner and nods his head.

"Over there," JJ adds. "He watched the soldiers and made the carving while hiding over there." JJ looks at the second stone.

"Yeah, that's a good spot, he could see everything from there," Calvin proclaims. Suddenly there is another dull thud against the solid rock wall as Brad keeps acting like a pitcher

"Let's pick a spot and check the maps out," JJ announces. Calvin nods his head.

"That flat section of the basin wall is only about five feet high, I'll land the drone, and since it's been a while, I need to call my dad," Calvin says as he looks over to Brad. "Hey, Brad I need to use your cell phone!" Calvin grabs the remote control and the takes over the flight of the drone. Steadily he lands it on the flat rock. In the background Brad is winding up as a pitcher and fires another rock against the wall with the same dull thud.

"Another strike, coach, I'm ready to go in!" Brad mutters

to himself. "Sure, I'll leave it next to your drone." Calvin and JJ are kneeling, checking out the maps. Brad walks up and places the cell phone by the drone.

"You guys got this? I've got a big game going," Brad asks as he walks back out into the ravine floor and resumes his pitching stance.

"I didn't notice this before, but that mountain looks like the carving on the second stone," JJ announces as he points to a mountain in the background. Calvin checks it out.

"You really couldn't see it good until we got here, and according to the map, that semi-flat is known as Miner's Needle Mountain," Calvin adds. JJ intently studies the paper map and the second stone map.

"The carving on the stone has some sort of marking in the upper left corner. Let's see if there's any correlation with the real mountain," JJ says. "How about flying the drone over so we can take a look?" Calvin nods his head and begins to operate the remote control. Within seconds the drone takes off and heads to Miner's Needle Mountain that's about a quarter of a mile away. The two boys diligently watch the monitor screen on the control panel. Meanwhile Brad is in his pitcher's stance. He winds up and fires off a rock that smashes against the rock wall with a loud, dull thud.

"Strike one!" Brad yells out as he gets back into his pitcher's stance. He winds up and fires a rock off with the same loud, dull thud.

"Strike two!" Brad yells out as JJ and Calvin keep their eyes fixed on the monitor screen. Suddenly JJ gets wide-eyed.

"Stop!" JJ yells out. "I think I saw something." The two boys intently stare at the monitor screen as Calvin directs the drone back to its pervious flight position. They exchange perplexed looks.

"Wow, there's a hole in the upper corner of the mountain that is the same as the markings on the stone, then the arrows point down to this ravine," JJ announces. Calvin nods his head.

"Yeah, and you can't see the hole in the mountain unless you're standing in the right spot," Calvin adds. "I'm bringing the drone back." JJ stares out to the mountain and up the ravine.

"Maybe, the circle on the stone map is the cave that's closed off by a pile of rock, which would indicate the smaller large circle inside the larger one," a curious JJ says. Calvin gives JJ a serious look as he lands the drone by the cell phone.

"JJ, it's starting to look like the secret cave is around here, but where?" a baffled Calvin says.

Meanwhile Brad starts his wind up, then holds his stance and scans the ravine to his left and to his right, like a pitcher checking the base runners.

"Okay, folks, Brad Thompson on the mound, the bases are loaded, and the count is three and two…and the Cubs are up by one. Thompson in the wind up…and he fires it in there," Brad says as he plays the announcers. Then the rock smashes into a bush not far from JJ and Calvin, but this time something was different.

"Strike three!" Brad shouts out. "Cubs win, Cubs win!" Brad is jumping for joy as JJ gives Calvin a suspicious look.

"Did you hear that?" a curious JJ ask. Calvin throws his hands up sporting a perturb look.

"What, Cubs win, please, we hear it all the time. It makes me hyperventilate because I don't know how loud he's going to get!" a disgruntled Calvin responds. JJ shakes his head.

"No, not that, the sound. The sound of the rock, it was different this time, listen," JJ says as he looks out toward Brad.

"Brad, do that again!" JJ asks. Brad gives JJ a head nod.

"Cubs win, Cubs win!" Brad yells out. JJ shakes his head.

"No, I mean throw the rock in the exact same spot," JJ replies. Brad tips his hat and sets up like a pitcher in his stance. He winds up and aggressively throws the rock toward the same bush. The rock hurls through the air and smashes into a large bush, generating the same hollow thud with a slight echo that had gotten JJ's attention in the first place. JJ gets wide-eyed and runs toward the bush. He quickly stops in front of the bush and curiously inspects it. JJ looks at Calvin and Brad.

"Over here, guys!" an anxious JJ says. Calvin and Brad rush up to JJ. Calvin gives JJ a puzzled look.

"What's up?" a curious Calvin asks. JJ points to the bush.

"Use your belts and separate this bush!" JJ commands. Calvin and Brad whip their belts off and position them through the center of the bush with each one having about half of the bush secured with their belt. Then they carefully start to pull on their belts, slowly separating the bush in the center. JJ intently stares as the bush as it gradually becomes two halves exposing a pile of rocks. The boys get wide-eyed and slack-jawed at their discovery.

"Wow, I can't believe it, that's the carving on the stone!" an excited JJ announces. Calvin gives JJ a look of suspense.

"JJ…I think we found the cave!" a jubilant Calvin replies as the boys stare at the pile of rocks in awe.

"Well, there's only one way to find out," JJ says as he looks at Brad. "Brad, cup your hands and give me a lift. Calvin, let's get the flashlight." Brad cups his hands as Calvin whips off his backpack and pulls out his flashlight. They share anxious looks as JJ nods his head to indicate he's ready to go. With the flashlight in his back pocket, he steps into Brad's cupped hands and straightens himself out.

"Brad, I need a couple of more feet," JJ announces. Brad nods his head.

"Sure, here you go," Brad replies as he muscles JJ up to about eight feet high to the rock pile. JJ looks down at Brad and gives him a nod.

"That should do it," JJ informs him. Then JJ carefully removes the top rock, about the size of a football, and carefully repositions the rock. With the top rock removed, JJ notices a small opening and grabs the flashlight from his back pocket. He gives Calvin and Brad an anxious look, then turns the flashlight on as he peeks inside the opening.

"Do you see anything?" a curious Calvin asks as Brad huffs and puffs.

"It's a cave all right and totally dark," JJ states.

"Hey, can you hurry up? Your cowboy boots are killing my hands!" Brad announces.

"Just hold on a little more," JJ requests as he scans the flashlight beam from side to side, slowly working the beam deeper and deeper into the cave. Then suddenly the flashlight beam reveals a bag of gold. JJ sports an anxious look as he keeps scanning the flashlight beam when it comes across dozens of bags with gold coins and nuggets. JJ gets wide-eyed and looks in awe.

"We found it!" an exuberant JJ announces as Calvin and Brad share elated smiles. "We found the secret cave of gold!" Then out of nowhere the sound of gunshots fills the ravine.

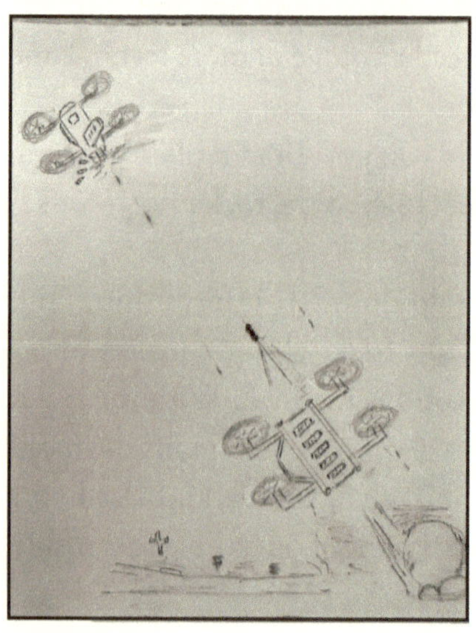

CHAPTER TEN

THE BATTLE

The boy's jubilation immediately turns to terror as bullets ricochet off the rock ledge next to the bush. Panic covers their faces as a hail of bullets continues to shower their position. JJ no sooner turns around when a bullet blasts the flashlight out of his hand. Calvin and Brad look bewildered and frightened and exchange confused looks as bullets kick up dirt right behind them.

"Gunshots, get me down from here!" a terrified JJ yells. Brad anxiously lowers JJ to the ground where the boys quickly crouch down and huddle together.

"We need to call for help, let's go!" JJ says as the boys quickly scamper back to the rock wall where the cell phone is located. They're panting hard and have taken cover, when suddenly the cell phone is blasted off the rock wall.

"My cell phone!" Brad yells. "What's going on?" JJ's lips get tight, and his eyes are tense.

"Somebody is shooting at us!" JJ states. Calvin looks up at the rock wall.

"My drone!" an anxious Calvin says as he quickly gets up and grabs his drone, then just as quickly ducks back down. The boys are scared and look bewildered by the events that have quickly unfolded upon them.

At the top of the basin, Sam has the binoculars in position and is looking down the ravine toward the boys' location. Next to Sam is Squeeze who is operating a drone remote control. Close to Squeeze is Boomer who is blasting away with two pistols, one in each hand as Rocco fires off his short-barreled revolver. Sam lowers the binoculars as his men continue to shoot round after round.

"Hold your fire, you're wasting ammo. Their protected by that rock wall," Sam commands as he gives Squeeze a serious look.

"Squeeze, swing the drone around and come up the ravine," Sam says as his eyebrows narrow and his face grows sinister.

"We'll flush them out like rats," Sam mutters to himself as he watches an intimidating black drone with an ammo clip and a short, smoking barrel fly off to its new position.

The boys are frightened and share desperate looks as they helplessly crouch down behind the ravine rock wall for cover. Brad flashes a determined look.

"I'm getting my cell phone!" Brad says as he quickly crawls out to get his cell phone. Suddenly gunshots ring out, and the ground around Brad kicks up from the bullets. Brad gets wide-eyed and hustles back for cover behind the rock wall.

"Look at my cell phone!" a disgruntled Brad cries out as he looks at a large bullet hole in the middle of his cell phone. Brad gives JJ and Calvin a serious look.

"Hey, I think I saw a drone shooting at me!" Brad announces. JJ and Calvin rear their heads back.

"A drone?" a puzzled JJ asks. Brad nods his head and points in the direction he saw the drone.

"Let me see," a curious Calvin responds. He finds a small ledge in the five-foot rock and positions his foot, then quickly lifts himself up and takes a quick peek over the rock ledge. Almost immediately a gunshot rings out with a bullet ricocheting off the top of the rock wall. Calvin crouches back down and gives JJ a frantic look.

"It's a drone all right, and it looks like it's headed down the first ravine!" an anxious Calvin announces. JJ and Brad share a worried look.

"We're sitting ducks if the drone turns up this direction!" JJ replies as he looks for a couple of rocks. He quickly gathers up two rocks and gives Calvin and Brad a serious look.

"We got to stop that drone from getting down here and making the turn!" JJ proclaims, then he quickly gets up and gives the two stones a rapid heave, one right after the other. JJ ducks back down as the boys watch the two rocks sail toward the drone. But neither rock even comes close to hitting the drone. Calvin and Brad give JJ a pathetic-looking stare.

"Dude, nice try, was that your Amy imitation?" a sarcastic Brad asks as JJ shakes his head.

"Whatever," JJ responds. Brad looks around for some rocks.

"Here, let me try," Brad says as he picks up three rocks. Then he quickly stands up and rapid-fires off the three rocks one right after the other. The boys watch as all three rocks barely miss the drone.

At the top of the ravine, Sam lowers the binoculars and rears his head back.

"Whoa, that kid has a cannon for an arm. Don't get too close," a surprised Sam says as his hit men gaze down toward the ravine. Sam confidently nods his head and looks at Rocco and Boomer.

"Rocco, Boomer, you two head down the ravine and

use that ledge on the rock wall. There's plenty of cover, and you should be able to sneak up on them," Sam orders. Rocco and Boomer nod their heads and put their weapons in their holsters.

"Okay, boss," Rocco responds as he walks down the basin toward the start of the ravine and the ledge on the rock wall. Boomer follows.

Meanwhile, the boys have no choice but to keep cover behind the rock wall as the situation seems to be getting more dire. They look desperate and frightened. JJ gives Calvin and Brad a serious look.

"If that drone comes up the ravine, we're in big trouble!" JJ announces. Calvin perks up and sports a confident look as he pushes his glasses up off his nose.

"It's time for the new special feature!" Calvin replies as JJ and Brad look puzzled.

"What's that?" Brad asks.

"You'll see," Calvin responds as he reaches into his backpack and pulls out two large four-inch-long with about a one-inch-diameter bottle rockets on twelve-inch launch sticks. JJ and Brad are a bit taken by surprise as they share a glance and a smile. They curiously watch Calvin as he slides the long bottle rocket stick into one of the cylindrical tubes attached to the side of the drone. He carefully twists the bottle rocket's fuse to an ignition wire, then methodically repeats the process with the second bottle rocket. Calvin brushes his hands together, then pushes his glasses up off his nose.

"Good to go…but we have one problem," Calvin states. JJ and Brad share a puzzled glance.

"Problem?" JJ asks as Brad throws his hand up, shaking his head.

"Oh great, somebody's trying to kill us, and we have another problem…like what?!" an irritated Brad responds. Calvin shrugs his shoulders.

"Well, to put it simply, I have no idea what's going to happen," Calvin says. JJ flashes a confused look.

"Like, what do you mean?" JJ asks. Calvin's eyebrows lower, and he rubs his chin as if he's in deep thought. He gives JJ a serious look.

"Let's just say, stuff like trajectory, distance…we only have two chances," Calvin explains. JJ nods his head and sports a serious look.

"Then I need to get over to that rock wall behind those boulders and get a view of the first launch," JJ proclaims as the boys look over to a group of large boulders at the end of the ravine rock wall. Calvin gives JJ a serious look.

"Yeah, but JJ, you got to run across that open area," a concerned Calvin says. JJ stares out toward the open area and flashes a determined expression.

"I know, but we only have two chances, and we need

the second one to count," an eager JJ responds. JJ gets ready to make the dangerous dash to the boulders, and he gives Brad a serious look.

"On three, Brad, fire off a couple of rocks toward the drone, ready…one, two, three!" JJ says as he takes off. Suddenly Brad grabs JJ's backpack and pulls him backward and gives JJ a stern look.

"I'll do it," Brad says. JJ looks puzzled at Brad's announcement.

"Brad, come on!" JJ replies as Brad shakes his head in defiance.

"No, I got this," Brad responds as JJ shakes his head. Brad grabs two rocks and gives JJ and Calvin a nod, then he quickly stands up and gives the rocks a strong heave one after the other.

"Here we go!" a determined Brad says as he takes off and runs across the open area much like a halfback in football. He zigzags as a hail of gunshots ring out and the ground near Brad's feet kick up from the bullets. He's giving it everything he's got to make it to the group of large boulders at the end of the rock wall. Bullets zing and ping all around Brad as he runs for his life. He continues his football moves as the group of boulders get nearer. Finally he runs up and gets behind a large boulder, letting out a big sigh of relief.

"Whoa, that was close!" an exhausted Brad mutters to himself. He looks over to JJ and Calvin with a big smile and gives them the thumbs-up. JJ and Calvin exchange a smile of relief and return the thumbs-up.

"He made it!" a relieved JJ says. "Okay, Calvin, it's time to fly!" Calvin looks determined as he operates the remote control and watches the drone lift off the ground.

Sam is scanning the ravine as he adjusts his binoculars when suddenly Calvin's drone appears from behind the rock wall and ascends into the sky. He lowers the binoculars and looks surprised as Squeeze watches the drone with a puzzled face.

"You're kidding me!" an irritable Sam says. Squeeze gives Sam a dumbfounded look.

"Boss, they have a drone!" Squeeze announces. Sam gives Squeeze a perturbed look.

"I can see that!" an angry Sam replies. "Blast it out of the sky!" he commands.

Squeeze frantically taps the remote-control knob that operates the drone's shooting frequency as Sam looks on with a mean expression.

Against a bright-blue background of sunny skies, the black drone and Calvin's drone face each other about forty yards apart. The black drone fires away with rapid muzzle blasts as spent shells fall from the bottom of the drone's body.

Calvin's drone hovers up and down as a desperate Calvin manipulates his machine the best, he can, to avoid taking any direct hits. The scene is tense as multiple bullet tracers zip past Calvin's drone.

At the bottom of the ravine, JJ takes a quick peek over the wall as Calvin aggressively operates the remote control. JJ scans the black drone and then checks out Brad's position. Suddenly a bullet ricochets off the top of the rock wall, and JJ quickly ducks down. He gives Calvin a serious look.

"Okay, Calvin, he's got an angle on it!" JJ announces.

At the top of the ravine, Sam continues to monitor the events as Squeeze pounds on the remote-control trigger switch. Sam pulls his pistol from the holster and fires off two shots at Calvin's drone. He gives Squeeze an anxious look.

"Come on, Squeeze, blast that pesky thing out of the sky!" a frustrated Sam yells. Squeeze gives Sam a hapless look.

"I will, boss, as soon as it stops moving!" Squeeze responds. Sam cringes and looks down toward the long ravine wall.

"Where's Rocco and Boomer?" an irritable Sam says. "Those two should be down in the ravine by now."

Somewhat out of view of Sam, Rocco and Boomer are creeping along the five-foot ledge on the rock wall that leads to the large boulders where Brad is positioned. The two make steady progress and remain unnoticed.

An occasional bullet continues to ricochet off the top of the rock wall, keeping JJ and Calvin crouched down for cover. The boys are getting anxious knowing that if the black drone makes the turn and heads up the ravine, they're in big trouble. Calvin nervously operates the remote control, then he gives JJ an encouraging look.

"I'm ready to launch—fire one!" Calvin announces with a confident grin.

Almost one hundred feet in the sky the two drones face off. The black drone continues to fire round after round as the muzzle flashes ignite the bright-blue sunny sky. Calvin's drone abruptly stops its up-and-down motion and holds a steady pattern. Then suddenly a bottle rocket blasts out from one of the long cylindrical tubes and streaks through the air heading straight for the black drone. All looks good when within a couple of seconds, the bottle rocket loses momentum and falls thirty feet short and ten feet below its target before harmlessly exploding.

At the top of the ravine, Sam lowers his binoculars and flashes a perturbed but surprised expression as he looks out toward the drones.

"Oh, so you want to play Fourth of July?" an angry Sam mutters out loud as he looks at Squeeze. "Blast that drone out of the sky, Squeeze!" Squeeze gives Sam a desperate look, then pounds the trigger button on the remote control. The hail of bullets and the echo of gunshots fill the ravine.

Meanwhile, Calvin looks beside himself as JJ blankly stares out toward the drones. Then JJ looks at Calvin.

"Calvin, that wasn't even close!" a worried JJ says. Calvin looks at JJ with a concerned expression.

"I need those corrections and fast!" Calvin replies.

Back at the boulders, Brad has just finished peeking at the first bottle rocket launch and looks over at JJ and Calvin. He cups his hands around his mouth.

"Take it thirty feet closer and ten feet higher!" Brad calls out but not too loud to give up his position. He sees JJ can't hear him, so he yells the corrections out in desperation.

"Hey, thirty feet closer and up ten!" Brad yells out against the sound of gunshots.

JJ gives Brad a puzzled look and quickly puts a hand to his ear gesturing he can't hear what Brad is saying as an anxious Calvin looks on.

"JJ, what's up?" Calvin asks. "I need those corrections!" JJ stares out toward Brad, then looks at Calvin.

"He's yelling something, but I can't hear him!" a puzzled JJ responds.

At the boulders, Brad can see by JJ's reactions that his message is not getting through, and he knows time is not on their side. Brad looks troubled and must think of something fast. Then Brad gets wide-eyed and looks confident that he has an idea that will work. With JJ looking on, Brad flashes both hands open three times and points forward. Then he flashes both hands open one time and points up. Brad repeats his hand gestures.

The situation is growing more tense and dire with each passing second. Bullets keep ricocheting off the top of the rock wall forcing JJ and Calvin to keep cover as Calvin is trying his best to navigate his drone to avoid the repeated blasts from the black drone. JJ looks out toward Brad and quickly realizes what Brad is doing as he repeats his hand gestures.

"Calvin, he's giving you the corrections…he's telling you to take the drone thirty feet closer and ten feet higher!" an excited JJ announces. Calvin flashes a big smile and gives JJ a head nod.

"Corrections completed!" an anxious Calvin replies as he pushes his glasses up off his nose.

In the battle of the skies, Calvin's drone hovers into

its new position as tracer bullets continue to streak by just missing Calvin's drone. JJ notices Brad is giving him the thumbs-up and confirms that Calvin has positioned his drone exactly where Brad wanted it. JJ gives Calvin an encouraging look.

"It's thumbs-up, Calvin—fire!" JJ yells out. Calvin quickly pushes the fuse ignition button.

"Fire two!" Calvin eagerly announces.

Calvin's drone is hovering in its new position when suddenly the last bottle rocket blasts out of the tube. The two drones face each other in aerial combat with bullets zipping past Calvin's drone as the bottle rocket streaks through the sky toward the black drone. The bottle rocket leaves a trail of smoke as it descends from its corrected ten feet elevation and arches directly toward the black drone.

It's a perfect shot as the bottle rocket strikes the drone and lodges into the ammo clip. Within seconds, the bottle rocket explodes, and then almost immediately the exploding bottle rocket creates a huge secondary explosion from the ammo clip. The explosion is intense and powerful as it blows up the black drone into pieces as it falls from the sky in a ball of fire.

JJ and Calvin are ecstatic and slap each other's hands. In the background, Brad fist pumps over his head as he jumps up and down.

"All right, we did it!" JJ and Calvin say together as they share big smiles.

At the top of the ravine, it's a different scene, with Sam and Squeeze both wide-eyed and slack-jawed at the events that just unfolded. Sam slowly brings the walkie-talkie to his mouth.

"Mack, can you read me?" a despondent Sam asks.

"Yeah, I can read you. Did you get them?" Mack replies. Sam sports a disappointed look.

"Ah…not quite. Look, Mack, I'll explain later, but we need a helicopter out here," Sam announces as his eyes search for Rocco and Boomer.

On the rock ledge right above Brad, Rocco and Boomer share a sinister smile as they watch Brad celebrate, totally unaware of what's about to happen. Then suddenly Boomer jumps off the ledge and immediately puts Brad in a head-lock. Brad is taken by surprise, and a struggle ensues. With Boomer's arm around Brad's neck, it's difficult for him to catch his breath.

Across the ravine, JJ and Calvin see what has just happened, putting an abrupt stop to their celebration. They look on in shock as Brad struggles against a much larger person. Then they see Rocco who is still standing on the rock ledge watching with a sinister smile, waiting to jump into the melee.

JJ and Calvin share a desperate glance, then quickly look back out toward Brad.

"Calvin, we got to help Brad!" an anxious JJ says. They share a head nod and take off running across the open ravine to Brad's location. But no sooner than they start to run, gunshots start to blast away with bullets zipping through the air and ricocheting off the rock wall. The two boys have no option but to quickly duck down for cover. Calvin gives JJ a worried look.

"JJ, what are we going to do?" a despondent Calvin cries out as JJ looks on feeling hopeless.

Back at the rock ledge and the boulders, Brad's struggles continue as Boomer tightens his grip. Boomer sports a mean face and leans over close to Brad's left ear.

"Listen, kid, the more you fight, the tighter this gets!" Boomer states as he muscles his arm around Brad's neck. Brad is not someone who quits, and he knows he must do something as his breathing difficulties keep getting worse. With his face turning red, he realizes he must act. Then suddenly Brad jams his right elbow with all his force into

Boomer's ribs. The blow causes Boomer to cringe in pain as he is totally caught by surprise.

"UGH!" Boomer moans out loud as Brad immediately feels the tension around his neck let up. Within a spit second, Brad recognizes he has an opportunity, and he takes it. He quickly grabs Boomer's right arm and performs a judo flip. Boomer flips over Brad and slams to the ground, smacking his head on a rock. Boomer is stunned and semi-unconscious as Rocco looks on.

"Stop right there, kid!" Rocco calls out as he reaches for his revolver. But Brad wastes no time, and before you know it, he turns around and pulls Rocco's legs forward by the heels. Rocco's legs fly into the air as he falls back, whacking his head on the rock wall and knocking him unconscious. Brad sees his opportunity and takes off just as Boomer starts to lift his head off the ground as he begins to get his wits together. At the exact moment Boomer is raising his chest off the ground, Brad steps on his chest and dashes away.

Brad is running full throttle across the open area as a hail of gunshots unloads with dirt kicking up at Brad's feet. He makes it across the danger zone, grabbing his tent backpack along the way, and runs up to JJ and Calvin as he pants hard to catch his breath.

"We got to get out of here!" an anxious Brad lets out. "Come on, let's go!" JJ takes a quick glance up the ravine.

"Quick, grab the gear and belts. We'll head up the ra-vine...Calvin!" JJ yells out.

"What?!" Calvin quickly responds as the boys make a mad dash to get away. JJ gives Calvin an eager look.

"Fly the drone over to Miner's Needle Mountain and find a way to the top!" JJ responds back. Calvin gives JJ a head nod as the boys sprint toward the end of the ravine about sixty yards away. They will make their way to the mountain where they hope to seek higher ground and hopefully buy some time.

Back at the boulders, Sam is standing with his hands on his hips in front of Rocco and Boomer. The two hit men are sitting on a couple of large rocks nursing their headaches. Boomer is just staring down at the ground avoiding eye contact with Sam as Rocco is busy rubbing the back of his head. Off to the side, Squeeze is tracking the boys with Sam's binoculars. Sam steps closer to Rocco and Boomer.

"You guys are pathetic!" a disgusted Sam shouts out as he gives Rocco a questionable look.

"What happened?" Sam asks. Rocco gives Sam a lame face.

"I don't know, boss, it happened so fast," Rocco replies weakly. Sam rears his head back.

"So fast?!" Sam responds with a perturbed look. He walks over in front of Boomer who looks up at Sam with a sheepish grin.

"These kids aren't normal, Sam. We're going to need some help," Boomer proclaims. Sam is looking peeved and just shakes his head.

"This is unbelievable," Sam mutters to himself as he continues to shake his head.

"Boss, I see them!" an excited Squeeze announces. "They're headed toward that mountain." Squeeze points toward Miner's Needle Mountain as he lowers his binoculars and adjusts them for a better view. In the distance JJ and Calvin are running toward the mountain followed by Brad with the larger tent backpack. Sam flashes a wry smile.

"Smart but foolish. We can't get to them, but they'll be trapped. We'll surround the mountain and let the helicopter finish them off," Sam proclaims with a sinister smile.

It's later in the afternoon, and at the top of the mountain, the boys are looking over the edge. JJ flashes a serious look as he nods his head.

"Just as I thought," JJ mutters out loud. Calvin gives JJ a curious look.

"What's that?" Calvin asks as JJ continues peer over the edge.

"There's one of those guys on each side of the mountain," JJ replies as Brad throws his hands up in the air.

"Well, now what are we going to do?" a curious Brad

asks.

"I was thinking we can send up smoke signals, but that might take too long," JJ replies. "Besides…look!" JJ points toward the southern horizon.

In the far southern horizon, a large dust storm lines the horizon and is traveling toward the boys' location.

The boys gaze out toward the southern horizon and the oncoming storm. Brad turns to JJ and Calvin.

"Too bad we can't fly off!" Brad says as he tucks his thumbs into his armpits and flaps his arms like wings. JJ sports a smile, but Calvin's eyes light up. He pushes his glasses up off his nose as his eyes look tense as if in deep thought. Then he gives JJ and Brad a serious look.

"Maybe we can!" Calvin announces. JJ flashes a puzzled expression.

"How? The storm will be here soon," a curious JJ asks.

Calvin sports a confident smile.

"We're going to glide off the mountain!" Calvin proclaims as the three boys peer over the edge of the mountain. JJ and Brad share a dubious glance, then look back over the edge. Calvin gives JJ and Brad an encouraging look.

"We're going to use the tent and build a giant kite. It will look like this," Calvin says as he grabs a long stick and starts to draw in the dirt. JJ and Brad watch intently, and after a few minutes, Calvin completes his sketch, which reveals a traditional kite-shaped pattern with three stick figures that are holding on to a crossbar running from side to side. The stick figure in the center is larger than the other two figures and has a line drawn from its foot to the tail of the kite. Calvin sports a confident smile as JJ and Brad stare at the drawing. Brad flashes a puzzled expression.

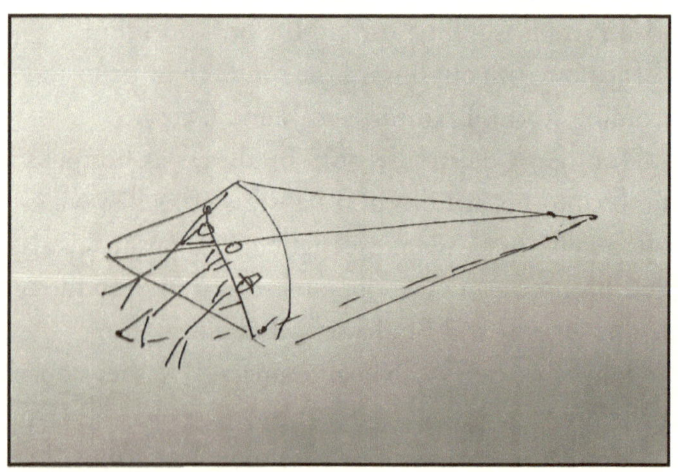

"So, why is the middle figure bigger?" a curious Brad asks. Calvin calmly nods his head.

"That's you. Since you're the biggest, you'll need to be in the center for balance," Calvin explains. "And the line from your foot to the tail is how we control the flight." Suddenly a gust of wind blows the drawing away as the boys share a glance.

"We better get busy," Calvin says as JJ and Brad nod their heads. In the background the line of dust on the horizon is larger and closer.

At the bottom of the mountain, Sam is getting antsy as he paces back and forth with one hand holding the binoculars in place and the other hand holding the walkie-talkie.

"I wonder what those rascals are up to?" Sam mutters to himself as he brings the walkie-talkie to his mouth.

"Chopper One, what's your position?" Sam demands as the walkie-talkie crackles.

"Sam, we're close…just west of you," the helicopter pilot responds. Sam anxiously looks westward with the binoculars, then lowers the binoculars and flashes a sinister smile.

"These kids have no chance, they're finished!" an angry Sam calls out.

An hour later at the top of the mountain, a large kite is propped off the ground resting on an extended crossbar. The kite is about fifteen feet long and ten feet wide from wing tip to wing tip. String ties the tent fabric to the tent poles, which make up the frame, and duct tape holds the tent poles together. The boys are staring at the kite, then Calvin pushes his glasses up off his nose and gives JJ a serious look.

"What about that guy at the bottom?" Calvin asks. "He's got a gun." JJ's eyebrows lower and his lips get tight as he looks around, then he spots a yucca plant and sports a big smile.

"I know, yucca bombs!" an excited JJ says. Brad rears his head back and gives JJ a puzzled look.

"Yucca bombs?" Brad replies as JJ points to the yucca plant.

"Yeah, we'll cut five yucca leaves, and you'll release them from the drone's claw," JJ explains.

"I like it, those spiky sword-shaped leaves with a spine tip will get his attention," an excited Calvin replies as he gives JJ the thumbs-up.

"The Spanish daggers, and once we release them…we jump," JJ adds. Brad looks skeptical as he peeks over the edge of the mountain.

"Jump?" an apprehensive Brad mutters to himself.

Several minutes have passed, and the wind is steadily getting stronger. The boys know they must act soon and have positioned themselves as drawn out by Calvin. JJ and

Brad are holding the kite over their heads as the wind ruffles the tent fabric. They have slipped their belt buckles through the crossbar and tied the belt straps around their chests for extra stability. Calvin ties a tent pole rope around Brad's right ankle and then gets busy tying the other end of the rope to the kite tail. On the ground near the mountain's edge is the drone with five yucca leaves held firmly by the drone's retractable claw.

"There, that should do it," Calvin announces as he finishes tying the rope to the kite's tail.

"Dude, do what?" a puzzled Brad asks. Calvin gives Brad a smile as he pushes his glasses up off his nose.

"It's simple. You move your right leg forward, we go up. You move your right leg back, we go down," Calvin explains as he picks up the remote control. Brad flashes a skeptical expression as he looks at JJ.

"Did you get that?" an anxious Brad asks. JJ shrugs his shoulder and gives Brad a light fist bump.

"You'll be fine, just follow directions," JJ responds as the drone lifts off the ground.

Meanwhile, Sam is looking at the mountain's edge through his binoculars, and then he looks in the opposite direction for the helicopter. He lowers the binoculars and sports a curious expression as he looks back up to the mountain's edge.

"What are they up to…and where's that helicopter?" Sam mutters to himself. Suddenly he flashes a curious face and quickly brings the binoculars to his eyes. In view through the binoculars, the drone is dive-bombing straight toward him. Sam lowers the binoculars and looks puzzled.

"Is that the pesky drone?" Sam mutters out loud as he raises the binoculars to his eyes.

"It's headed right toward me!" a surprised Sam says as he reaches for his pistol. Suddenly he lowers the binoculars and flashes a bewildered look.

"What's that thing carrying?" a curious Sam says as he brings the binoculars to his eyes for another look.

"You're kidding me…a drone with yucca leaves?!" a puzzled Sam responds as he lowers the binoculars. "What do they think they can do with this thing?" Sam says as he takes aim and fires, but the pistol jams.

In the sky the drone is streaking down like a dive bomber directly at Sam. Then suddenly the claw releases the five yucca leaves, much like the bombs from a fighter airplane in a World War II movie. In an instant the drone pulls up as the sharp-pointed yucca leaves zip through the air right toward their target.

A startled Sam throws his pistol to the ground in frustration, then helplessly looks up to the five yucca leaves that are screaming right at him. Within seconds and almost simultaneously, the yucca leaves slam to earth, sticking into the ground landing to his left, right, in front, and directly behind him. Sam looks beside himself as he sees the yucca leaves have surrounded him. Then suddenly the fifth yucca leaf plunges directly into Sam's foot.

"Ahhh!" Sam yells out. "My foot!" Sam anguishes in pain.

At the top of the mountain, the boys are ready to jump. They double-check the belt straps around their chests and grab the crossbar with strong grips as the wind continues to blow, ruffling the kite fabric. The boys share a glance and a quick head nod, then Calvin tosses the remote control to the ground.

"With the strong tail wind, we should make it all the way to the parking lot," an optimistic JJ says. Calvin gives Brad a serious look.

"Brad, whatever you do, keep your right leg forward as soon as we jump!" Calvin instructs. "I'll explain the rest as we go." Brad gives Calvin a dubious look.

"I'm kind of having a hard time with the jump-off part," an anxious Brad announces. JJ and Calvin flash a thumbs-ups.

"Okay, together on three…one, two, three—jump!" Calvin commands. They don't hesitate and instantaneously jump off the edge of the mountain. But immediately the kite plummets straight toward the ground. The boys hold on to the kite's crossbar in desperation as panic covers their faces. Their belts are stretched to the max, and the kite fabric is flapping wildly and loudly. The situation is dire, and time is quickly running out as the mountain's steep, vertical cliff is only about nine hundred feet. The boys are wide-eyed with looks of sheer terror as their legs uncontrollably flap as they fall headfirst. Calvin gives Brad a desperate but stern look.

"Brad!" Calvin screams out. "Move your right leg forward!" Brad gives Calvin a blank stare.

"Whoa! Whoa!" Brad yells. "We're going to crash!" JJ gives Brad an eager look.

"Brad!" JJ yells as Brad gives JJ the same blank stare.

"Oh no!" Brad yells. "We're going to die!" JJ grabs Brad's shoulder.

"Brad, move your right leg forward!" JJ yells out as he shakes Brad by the shoulder. Brad looks at JJ and then takes a quick glance toward the fast-approaching ground and back to JJ.

"What are we going to do?" a panic Brad asks.

"Move your right leg forward and now!" JJ firmly replies. Brad finally responds and slowly begins to move his right leg forward. And just as Calvin planned, the rope starts to tighten and slowly pulls the tail down. The kite gradually levels off and begins a normal but bumpy glide as the warm desert air provides an updraft, lifting the kite to the sky. The boys are all smiles and share a look of relief.

"Whew, that was close!" JJ proclaims as he gives Brad a smile and a pat on the back.

"Keep it steady, Brad, you're doing good," Calvin says. Brad flashes a big smile as the kite glides through the air with an occasional scattered cloud in front of them, but in the background the looming dust storm is picking up speed.

Meanwhile at the bottom of the mountain, Sam is pulling the yucca leaf out of his shoe. He looks up toward the kite as he tosses the yucca leaf and brings the walkie-talkie to his mouth.

"Chopper One, Chopper One, can you read me?" an agitated Sam asks as the walkie-talkie crackles.

"What's up, Sam?" the helicopter pilot replies.

"Look, there's a large kite heading in your direction… Shoot it down!" Sam commands.

"Roger, Sam, we see it…over," the helicopter pilot responds.

The boys continue their bumpy but steady glide. All seems well as their eyes enthusiastically search the ground and its spectacular views. The boys share a smile when suddenly

Brad gets wide-eyed.

"Hey look, there's a helicopter!" an excited Brad announces. In view from the west, a helicopter is traveling straight toward their location as they watch the helicopter with fixed eyes.

"It's coming this way," a curious Calvin says as JJ takes a double look at the helicopter.

"Yeah, like straight toward us!" an anxious JJ adds. "Geez, start waving, I don't think they see us!" The boys frantically wave to get the helicopter pilot's attention, but the fast-approaching helicopter is not veering off course and heading straight toward the kite.

"Dudes, they're not moving!" an excited Brad says as he continues to wave aggressively.

"Calvin, we need to get out of the way and fast!" a desperate JJ yells out. Calvin flashes a serious expression.

"Look, I'll shift my weight to the right, hold on, here we go!" Calvin announces as he shuffles his hands and moves out on the crossbar. With the change in balance, the kite dips down toward the right. Then Calvin quickly shuffles back into his original position and the kite levels, resuming its normal flight pattern. But unexpectedly the boys notice the helicopter veers to the left and is in a head-on flight pattern with the kite.

"Whoever is flying that thing is coming right at us. Hold on!" an anxious JJ yells out.

Within a split second, the helicopter streaks past the kite, barely missing the boys. Suddenly a blast of turbulent air hits the kite, flipping it over and causing the kite to tumble over several times out of control. The boys hold on for their lives as their legs flop wildly and terror covers their faces.

"Help!" Brad screams out in panic.

"Hold on, whatever you do!" Calvin advises.

"Whoa, whoa!" JJ yells out as the kite flips over a couple of more times, but then the kite stops flipping over and starts to rock back and forth, eventually returning to a steady glide.

"Wow!" Calvin says as he pushes his glasses up off his nose and searches for any damage.

"That guy nearly killed us!" an upset Brad says as he makes sure to keep his right leg straight.

"He did that on purpose!" an angry JJ calls out as he turns his head searching for the helicopter. Suddenly JJ gets wide-eyed.

"I think he's coming back!" a concerned JJ announces as the thumping noise of the helicopter gets louder.

From behind the kite, a black Huey helicopter makes a sharp banking turn and quickly positions itself along the side of the kite, then the side door slides open. In the doorway a gunman who is wearing a helmet and dark sunglasses is holding a long rifle. On the tail of the helicopter, the company name reveals GORGE MINING 1. Then the man with the rifle takes aim, and within a split second, a hail of bullets pours out toward the kite.

The boys desperately hold on to the crossbar as multiple bullets zip through the kite fabric as sparks fly off the crossbar. Gunshots and the thumping sound of the helicopter fill the air. The boys' mission of good will has turned into a perilous and dangerous adventure as they find themselves totally defenseless.

"Oh no!" Calvin screams out. "They're shooting at us!" More gunshots ring out as bullets zip through the kite creating multiple holes letting through scattered beams of sunlight. Suddenly a bullet strikes Calvin's belt loop, ripping it to pieces. Almost immediately Calvin starts to lose his grip and finds himself desperately dangling from the crossbar with one hand. JJ and Brad look on in horror.

"Help!" Calvin cries out. "I don't think I can hold on much longer!" Calvin's fingers slowly lose their grip as he struggles to hold on, but he can't maintain his grip and starts to fall. Suddenly Brad reaches out, and within a split second, he catches Calvin under his forearm.

"I gotcha, Calvin, don't worry!" Brad says as he holds on to Calvin. But the rapid weight change has thrown the kite out of balance, and it starts to descend, wobbling out of control. For Brad, his only concern is saving his best friend. So Brad uses only one arm and slowly lifts Calvin closer and closer to the crossbar. He exerts all his strength as his face shows the tension.

"Get your arms over the crossbar!" Brad yells out. Calvin responds and grabs the crossbar, and with Brad's help, he gets both of his arms over the crossbar, securing his safety.

The boys look frightened but relieved as they slowly regain control of the kite. Then there is another round of gunshots as more bullets rip through the kite fabric. With the damage from the bullets and the pressure of the air under the kite, the small holes begin to tear, creating larger holes throughout the kite fabric. The large tears are causing the kite to lose airborne stability on top of the attackers in the helicopter who are now flying behind the kite.

"Dudes, we're going down!" an anxious Brad yells. JJ gives Calvin a serious look.

"We've got to do something. We're sitting ducks!" a nervous JJ calls out.

"JJ, you and I swing sideways, and Brad, move your leg back and forth!" Calvin commands. The boys quickly conduct their maneuvers, and within no time the kite starts to weave up and down as it glides left to right.

Back in the helicopter, the pilot, who is wearing a flight helmet and dark sunglasses turns around to the gunman.

"Hey, let's get this over with!" the pilot demands. The gunman nods, then pulls down a large black machine gun from the interior roof of the helicopter. The gunman takes position behind the large weapon, then cocks the side bolt and takes aim. There is a loud burst of machine gun fire toward the kite, and spent bullet shells fly from the weapon. Tracer rounds just miss the kite but give the gunman the adjustments he needs as he fixes the sites. The gunman confidently nods his head with the kite doomed in the gun's sites.

Suddenly two FBI Apache attack helicopters fly up along each side of the Gorge Mining 1 helicopter. Then the multibarrel 20mm cannon gun under the cockpit rotates and takes aim directly at the Gorge chopper. The pilot's window slides open on the Apache chopper, and the pilot puts his hand out the window pointing down, a signal for the Gorge chopper to land.

The gunman on the Gorge chopper turns the machine gun around and raises his hands over above his head as the Gorge helicopter begins to descend.

The boys are unaware of the activity behind them as JJ and Calvin continue to swing from side to side and Brad moves his leg in a back-and-forth motion. The kite is gradually losing altitude as the tears in the kite get bigger and bigger and the wind gets stronger and stronger. The boys fear the kite will suddenly tear wide open, plunging them to the ground. Then on the left side of the kite, the Apache helicopter slowly flies alongside the boys' kite. They share looks of apprehension as the Apache chopper moves forward.

"Oh no!" Brad screams out. "Here they come again!" JJ takes a double look and realizes it's the FBI and not the Gorge chopper, and he gets wide-eyed.

"Wait, look, it's the FBI!" an enthusiastic JJ calls out as the Apache chopper flies along the side of the boys' kite. The pilot gives the boys a friendly wave as the boys share a smile and break out in cheers.

"Yeah!" the boys yell out. "All right!" the cheers continue. The boys are much relieved, so JJ and Calvin stop their swinging motion and Brad stops with the leg movement as the kite begins to level off and transition into a straightforward but bumpy glide.

Inside the Apache cockpit, the pilot wears a white helmet with the letters FBI in yellow across the front. He also wears dark aviator glasses as he adjusts the microphone that's attached to the helmet.

"Ground operations, this is FBI Chopper One, can you read me?" the pilot asks.

In the parking lot, FBI Agent Claymore, who is about fifty years old with a crew cut and wearing a black business suit, brings a walkie-talkie to his mouth. Anxiously waiting, the boys' parents huddle near Agent Claymore. In the background are the parents' vehicles along with two black Ford Expedition SUVs with yellow FBI lettering. An agent opens the rear door of one of the FBI vehicles and guides Mack, who is in handcuffs, into the back seat.

"This is Agent Claymore, over!" Agent Claymore replies as the parents nervously look on and mumble among themselves.

"We're about a mile out and have intercepted a helicopter along with detaining four individuals on the ground, over," the pilot informs him. Agent Claymore nods his head, then flashes a serious look.

"Good work…what about the boys?" a curious Agent Claymore asks as the parents' stare at Agent Claymore, deadpan, waiting for news. The walkie-talkie crackles.

"I'm seeing three boys who are gliding your way under a large kite. They appear okay, but the kite is pretty shot up," the pilot announces. "Actually, it's amazing they're still flying, hope they can make it." Agent Claymore turns to the parents; he gives them an encouraging but curious look.

"Folks, the boys are okay and headed in this direction… via a large kite," Agent Claymore states to the anxious parents who look relieved but confused. Then unexpectedly the walkie-talkie crackles again.

"Agent Claymore, can you read me?" the pilot asks. Agent Claymore looks surprised and brings the walkie-talkie to his mouth.

"Claymore, over," Agent Claymore responds.

"We're going to have to break contact, there's a huge dust storm with dangerous winds approaching exceptionally fast. The boys are about a half mile out and will be on their own, over," the pilot informs.

Abruptly the Apache helicopter makes a sudden bank turn and flies away. Underneath the kite the boys apprehensively watch the helicopter fade away as the kite aggressively starts to bounce from the wind. The kite is riddled with bullet holes and large tears on both front sides and the tail section with minimal, if barely, any fabric holding air. Suddenly JJ gets wide-eyed.

"Hey look!" an excited JJ says. "The parking lot!" In view are vehicles with flashing lights and people standing together next to one of the vehicles.

The kite begins to start to shake violently from the turbulent wind from the dust storm that is only a couple of hundred yards behind them. The boys start to wildly bounce around as they desperately hold on to the crossbar.

"How are we going to land this thing?" a worried Brad asks. Calvin gives JJ and Brad a serious look.

"We can't land it in this wind!" Calvin proclaims as the kite takes a strong jolt from a gust of wind.

"We're going to have to jump, untie your belt, Brad, and let's get ready!" JJ announces.

The kite is quickly approaching the parking lot, which is now less than a quarter of a mile away. The boys know their only chance is to jump on the flat surface of the parking lot. But the kite is rapidly descending with huge, jagged boulders below and the massive wall of dust close behind them. Then something amazing happens. A hint of a large image of Inka's face appears in the wall of dust, and almost like a miracle, what looks like a hand protrudes from the storm under the kite as if it's guiding the kite and the boys to their destination. The boys only have about a couple of hundred yards to the parking lot. They're violently bouncing around with hardly any kite fabric left. The boys know the situation is dire, then JJ gives Calvin and Brad a somber look.

"Just in case…brothers forever," JJ proclaims as Calvin and Brad give JJ a somber expression and nod their heads.

"Forever!" Calvin and Brad reply together. The boys share a smile and then look straight ahead with fixed eyes as the ground rushes past them.

"Okay. Jump!" JJ calls out. In sync, the boys let loose of the crossbar and hit the ground hard. They tumble several times before stopping, sitting up shaken but unharmed.

"Wow!" Calvin cries out. "We made it!" The boys get up off the ground and brush the dirt off as the parents quickly run up to their respective child. Agent Claymore walks up to the group and watches the parents fondly greet the boys.

"Calvin, you had us worried sick when you didn't text!" Tom Jackson, Calvin's dad, says as Calvin hugs his mom.

"I can explain, Dad!" Calvin replies as JJ's dad, Dan Garcia, brings Agent Claymore over to JJ for an introduction as they share a smile.

"JJ, this is FBI Agent Claymore," Dan says. JJ shakes the Agent Claymore's hand as debris starts to blow around the parking lot.

"Nice to meet you, sir," JJ replies, then JJ's dad gives him a stern look.

"Agent Claymore contacted me regarding the JJ Garcia Group. After a brief conversation, we realized you boys were in imminent danger," Dan says. JJ gives his dad a serious look.

"We didn't know we would be in danger; we were just trying to help a friend!" an apologetic JJ responds. Agent Claymore nods his head, then addresses the group.

"The FBI has been watching Gorge Mining and Mr. Jones for some time. But let me ask you, JJ, how were you boys going to help your friend out in this wilderness?" a curious Agent Claymore asks.

"My friend gave me two stone maps," JJ says as Agent Claymore flashes a puzzled expression.

"Stone maps?" a confused Agent Claymore asks. JJ, Calvin, and Brad share a glance.

"Yeah, maps to a secret cave of gold!" Calvin says as the parents exchange bewildered looks.

"Well, did you find this secret cave?" a curious Agent Claymore asks. Brad steps forward.

"We found it, and the treasure was inside!" Brad adds as his mom gives him a dubious look. Agent Claymore's eyes scan the boys, then he nods his head.

"Hmm…JJ, how about if you boys give my agents the stone maps and let them verify this cave?" Agent Claymore suggests. JJ gives Agent Claymore a serious look.

"Does my friend's people get to keep the gold?" JJ questions. Agent Claymore gives JJ a smile and nods his head.

"If my agents actually recover this gold, I'll personally make those arrangements," Agent Claymore states. The boys exchange apprehensive looks, then they huddle together and quietly talk among themselves. After a moment they nod their heads in agreement, and JJ gives Agent Claymore a serious look.

"It's a deal, but we'll give you the directions, and we keep the stone maps," a confident JJ offers to Agent Claymore. Agent Claymore nods his head in agreement, and the two shake hands. Agent Claymore looks out toward the incoming storm and then addresses the parents.

"Look, folks, this storm is getting intense. I would like to see everybody in my office at ten a.m. this Monday…if that works?" Agent Claymore announces. The parents share a glance, then nod their heads.

"Good, I'll see you all then," Agent Claymore says as he walks away. "Boy, do these kids have an imagination,"

Agent Claymore mutters to himself.

The storm is closing in, dust and debris are blowing all around, and the wind is howling as the parents scamper to their vehicles followed by the boys. Then JJ suddenly stops and gazes out toward the storm. He curiously squints his eyes and takes a double look but can't believe his eyes. He sees Inka standing at the base of the wall of dust, which appears to have stopped moving. JJ inquisitively just stares out at Inka whose long black hair is blowing in the wind. But it's obvious that only JJ can see or hear Inka's voice in his mind.

"Thank you, my brave warrior. And remember, I will always love you," Inka says. Calvin and Brad rush up to JJ and see he is mesmerized by something. Brad places his hand on JJ's shoulder and gives him a gentle shake.

"Dude, what is it, do you like dust storms or something?" Brad sarcastically asks. "Come on." Calvin gives JJ a serious look.

"Yeah, JJ, we got some unfinished business, let's go!" Calvin adds. JJ shakes his head as if he's back to reality and gives Calvin and Brad a stern look.

"You're right, we got some unfinished business. We need to get that gold to Inka's people so they can win the bid," JJ proclaims as the boys start to dash away toward the vehicles. JJ turns his head and looks out toward the storm. A somber expression covers his face as he sees the storm moving but no Inka.

FBI

ARIZONA DIVISION

Chapter Eleven

PROPHECY FULFILLED

It's Monday morning, and Agent Claymore is sitting at his desk with his hands together. Across from him sitting in a chair is Chief Kentoeka, a gentleman in his mid-sixties. He is the tribal leader of the Arizona Hopi Nation. He is dressed in blue jeans and a white long-sleeve cotton shirt with a vest. He is also wearing a cowboy hat and dons a large turquoise necklace. His two associates stand slightly behind him, one on each side. Agent Claymore looks at Chief Kentoeka, and he smiles as his hands abruptly separate.

"Well, Chief Kentoeka, that's the story. Stone maps, a secret cave of gold, and the boys insist your people get the money from it," Agent Claymore says with a slight chuckle. Chief Kentoeka smiles and patiently nods his head.

"It's a tough one to believe, but my field agents are searching the area as we speak. Anyhow, one way or another, we will know something very soon," Agent Claymore concludes. The phone rings, and Agent Claymore answers the phone.

"Great, have them come in," Agent Claymore says as he smiles at Chief Kentoeka.

The office door opens, and JJ, Calvin, and Brad enter the room followed by their parents. They walk up to the desk and stand behind three empty chairs located in front of the desk but slightly off-center. Agent Claymore addresses the group as Chief Kentoeka stands up to meet the group.

"Glad you folks could make it. I'd like to introduce you to Chief Kentoeka, he is the tribal leader of the Arizona Hopi Nation, and these two gentlemen are his associates," Agent Claymore announces as he looks at JJ.

"This young man is JJ Garcia," Agent Claymore adds. JJ smiles and shakes Chief Kentoeka's hand. Agent Claymore smiles at Calvin and Brad.

"And these are his friends, Calvin and Brad," Agent Claymore continues. Chief Kentoeka smiles at the parents and then sports a profound expression.

"It's a great honor to meet three living legends," Chief Kentoeka announces. The boys exchange puzzled glances as the parents rear their heads back looking bewildered. The parents quickly begin to mumble among themselves. Agent Claymore appears to be taken totally off guard and looks quite puzzled. He gives Chief Kentoeka a very strange, baffled look.

"Excuse me, Chief Kentoeka, did you say…living legends?" a confused Agent Claymore says. Meanwhile, the parents, who are still bewildered, have stopped mumbling and with blank faces stare at Chief Kentoeka waiting for his response. Chief Kentoeka gestures for the boys to sit down. The boys find a chair with JJ in the middle. All eyes are on Chief Kentoeka as the group anxiously waits for Chief Kentoeka to speak. He smiles at the group.

"Please, let me tell you a story that my people have passed down from generation to generation," Chief Kentoeka begins with fixed eyes from the group.

"Hundreds of years ago, a young princess known as Inka spoke of three boys who traveled from another time after being caught in a magical dust storm," Chief Kentoeka explains as Agent Claymore flashes a dubious expression. Chief Kentoeka continues the story.

"The boys arrived at the village during a vicious attack from a group of Spanish conquistadors," Chief Kentoeka continues with the story as Calvin's dad looks extremely puzzled.

"Spanish conquistadors!" a confused Tom says. "That's over five hundred years ago!" Tom scratches his head as Chief Kentoeka smiles and nods his head, then continues.

"Yes, that is true. The soldiers came to the village looking for the two fabled gold medallion necklaces that when place side-by-side revealed the directions to a secret cave of Spanish gold," Chief Kentoeka explains as Agent Claymore rubs the back of his head and flashes suspicious eyes.

"Oh brother!" Agent Claymore mutters to himself as Chief Kentoeka continues.

"Each boy had a special skill, and together they miraculously saved the village. It was then Princess Inka fell in love with her warrior," Chief Kentoeka says as Calvin and Brad give JJ a soft elbow nudges, but JJ could only sport a somber smile thinking of Inka. JJ's mom and dad share puzzled expressions and then look at JJ as Chief Kentoeka continues the story.

"Inka knew they had a destiny, so she gave her warrior stone copies of the maps. She knew someday he would help her people," Chief Kentoeka proclaims as the parents look on totally mesmerized. JJ's dad raises his hand.

"Excuse me, Chief Kentoeka, so whatever happened to the gold medallion necklace?" a curious Dan asks. The parents shift their eyes back to Chief Kentoeka, waiting for a response.

"About two hundred years ago, they were lost," Chief Kentoeka informs them as Dan rears his head back.

"Lost?!" Dan abruptly questions.

"Yes, and the only maps that exist would be the stone copies given to the boys by Inka," Chief Kentoeka explains. The parents start to mumble among themselves, but Agent Claymore can't take it anymore and reacts by erratically throwing his arm up.

"Okay, let me get this straight, what you're telling us is… these boys might have in their possession the stone maps in a story that's over five hundred years old, is that correct?" a doubtful Agent Claymore asks. Chief Kentoeka flashes a gentle smile and nods his head.

"That is correct. If these boys truly have in their possession the stone copies to the secret cave, then they are the boys in Inka's story," Chief Kentoeka explains as he looks at the boys and then the parents. "A story known as the Legend of Inka's Warriors." The room becomes dead quiet, then, suddenly the parents resume their mumbling to each other as Agent Claymore shakes his head and gives Chief Kentoeka a contemptuous look.

"With all due respect, Chief Kentoeka, but I find this all very hard to believe," Agent Claymore states. Then suddenly the phone rings, and everyone just stares at the phone… and then it rings again. Agent Claymore quickly grabs the phone and answers the call.

"Agent Claymore, FBI," Agent Claymore states. Then he gets wide-eyed and looks beside himself. "Can you repeat that… Well, I be… Thank you," Agent Claymore responds. He hangs up the phone and looks at Chief Kentoeka with a big smile.

"Congratulations, Chief Kentoeka!" Agent Claymore yells out. "My agents have found the cave, and it's filled with bags of gold!" The boys are ecstatic and jump to their feet as the room breaks out in pandemonium. Chief Kentoeka gives the boys a big smile.

"With the powers granted to me, I welcome you boys to the Hopi Nation!" Chief Kentoeka announces as the applause fades to a stop. Then Chief Kentoeka places his hand in a fist-up position on the desk and gestures for Calvin to do the same. Calvin eagerly responds and places his fist on top of Chief Kentoeka's hand.

"Calvinteeka, I'm an Eagle scoutmaster, and I award you the merit badge of Citizenship in the Community," Chief Kentoeka proclaims. Calvin's eyes light up, and he gives his parents a big smile and pushes his glasses up off his nose. Chief Kentoeka then gestures for Brad to follow. Brad places his fist on top of Calvin's fist as Chief Kentoeka gives Brad a serious look.

"Bradtoeka, I'm a student of the martial arts, and I would be honored to tell your sensei you are ready to earn your first-degree black belt," Chief Kentoeka announces as Brad looks at his mom and silently mouths the word, "Dad." Brad's mom covers her mouth with one hand, much like an expression of joy. Finally. Chief Kentoeka gestures to JJ with a soft smile. JJ then gets ready to place his fist in position on Brad's fist.

"And to Inka's soul mate, JJkatoe," Chief Kentoeka says as he looks at JJ's dad. "I will arrange for my associates to purchase two dozen of your finest horses." JJ's dad gets wide-eyed and slack-jawed from the offer. Chief Kentoeka gives JJ a serious look.

"And, JJkatoe, please teach our young to ride like the wind," Chief Kentoeka requests. JJ nods his head and sports a somber smile as he places his fist on top of Brad's fist. Chief Kentoeka addresses the group.

"Ladies and gentlemen, it's my privilege to present to you…Inka's Warriors," Chief Kentoeka proclaims.

"To Inka and her Warriors," JJ says in a soft tone. "I know you're here, Inka, I can feel your spirit," JJ says very quietly to himself. Then something miraculous happens, with Chief Kentoeka's and the three boys' fist on the desk, Inka's semitransparent hand with the turquoise bracelet around her wrist gently covers JJ's hand. JJ smiles as he knows Inka is present, and they have fulfilled their destiny.

The End

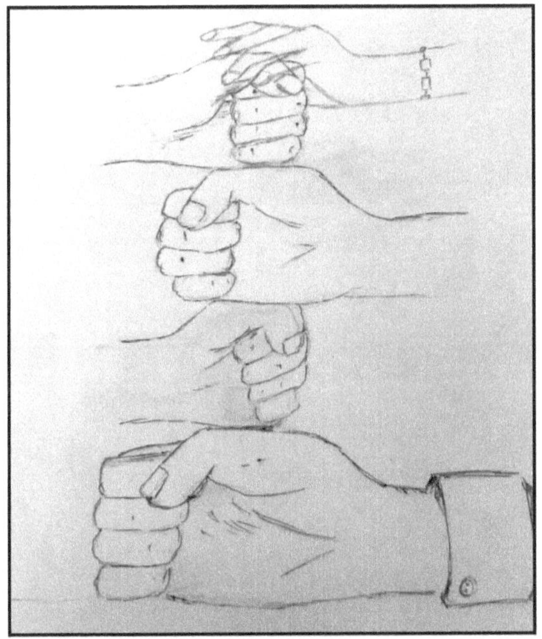